ADELE GRIFFIN

Witch Twins

at Camp Bliss

ILLUSTRATIONS BY

Jacqueline Rogers

HYPERION PAPERBACKS FOR CHILDREN

NEW YORK

For Tessa and Tanya

Text copyright © 2002 by Adele Griffin
Illustrations copyright © 2002 by Jacqueline Rogers
All rights reserved. No part of this book may be reproduced or transmitted in any form or by any means, electronic or mechanical, including photocopying, recording, or by any information storage and retrieval system, without written permission from the publisher. For information address Hyperion Books for Children, 114 Fifth Avenue, New York, New York 10011-5690.

First Hyperion Paperback edition, 2003
3 5 7 9 10 8 6 4 2
Printed in the United States of America

Library of Congress Cataloging-in-Publication Data
Griffin, Adele.
Witch twins at Camp Bliss / Adele Griffin.— 1st ed.
p. cm.
Summary: When the ten-year-old witch twins head for summer camp, Claire is excited and Luna is reluctant, but things do not turn out quite the way either of them expects.
ISBN 0-7868-0763-6 (tr.) — ISBN 0-7868-1583-3 (pbk.)
[1. Twins—Fiction. 2. Sisters—Fiction. 3. Camps—Fiction.
4. Witches—Fiction. 5. Virginia—Fiction.] I. Title
PZ7.G W 2002
[Fic]—dc21   2001051760

Visit www.hyperionchildrensbooks.com

for
Megan —
have fun!

Joseph Bruchac

Contents

1
Who Needs Zest?

"I T'S HOT ENOUGH TO SLAP your grandmother!" exclaimed Claire Bundkin to her identical twin sister, Luna. They were sitting together on the outdoor platform of the Philadelphia train station, waiting for the northbound local.

Luna frowned. "Claire, that's not a very nice expression," she said. "Especially since we're about to see our very own grandmother in less than an hour." She waved her folded-paper fan in front of her warm face and sighed.

"It's hot enough to kick a nun," Claire responded. "Hot enough to punch the post-man!"

Luna's frowned deepened. She did not like thinking about kicked nuns and punched postpeople, but it was too hot to argue. Besides, she felt uncomfortable enough from the dose of greasy sunscreen that their mother had rubbed into every exposed inch of her skin earlier that morning. "You'll thank me later. Most permanent sun damage occurs before age twenty," Jill Bundkin had warned. (Their mother, who was a doctor, knew a lot of grim medical statistics.)

To Luna, who was ten, twenty seemed too old to bother thinking about. Twenty was years past the most important things, like becoming a teenager or getting her ears pierced. And it was way, way past the next five weeks that she would be spending at Camp Bliss.

There was no turning back now. In less than twenty-four hours, their grandmother would be driving the twins all the way down to Bluefly, Virginia, to spend one whole month plus one week at camp. Their mother was on call at the hospital this weekend; otherwise she would have taken them. Their father, a newspaper reporter, was in California on special assignment.

Neither twin had ever been to camp. But both girls had spent hours studying the Camp Bliss pamphlet trying to get the idea of it. They imagined themselves galloping over the "rolling green fields," playing tennis on the "professional, all-clay courts," stitching bead belts during "freestyle crafts time," and, most important, making friends with other campers, "girls ranging from ages eight to fourteen."

When it had been months away, Camp Bliss had seemed like fun to Luna. Now she was dreading it. Why had she ever thought camp would be a good idea? First, she did not like to venture off to new, strange places. Second, she was not very talented at sports, especially sports that involved balls, rackets, and nets. Last and worst, she was not that good at making new friends. She could never come up with the funny joke or the right questions that broke the ice.

In fact, she figured that except for maybe some talent at belt-beading, she would be all-around blah at Camp Bliss.

The train pulled into the station.

"Air-conditioning!" yelled Claire with relief as she leaped through the door and shinnied into her seat, feet up with her back against the window. She pointed. "Go across, not next."

"Duh-uh." Luna huffed as she took her seat across the aisle. It was too hot to sit next to her sister, or anyone else. She put her overnight bag in the empty seat, so that nobody else would make the mistake of sitting *next*, either.

"Whew!" Claire lolled her tongue and panted like a dog. "I'm glad our trunks were sent ahead to Virginia. I would pass out if I had to pick up anything heavier than a glass of iced tea."

"Think of poor Justin," Luna reminded

her. Their older brother, Justin, had been hired for his very first summer job working as a grocery delivery boy. He told them he needed to gain some muscles if he wanted to try out for eighth-grade football next year. So far, Justin had lost two pounds. He blamed it on too much sweating.

"I'll get it back in million-dollar biceps," he told his sisters. "When you come home from your girlie-girl camp next month, you won't even recognize this guy. And it'll cost each of you five bucks if you want me to carry up your junk from the car."

Five weeks was such a huge amount of time to be away, Luna thought. Justin probably would be unrecognizable when they returned. The longest she and Claire had ever been away from home had been last summer, when they had gone fishing with their father on Orange Clam Island for two weeks. Even then, they'd had at least one parent, in case of emergency.

Camp Bliss had no parents. Just kids and counselors.

"I hope Mom won't be too lonely without us," Luna said quietly. "Maybe one of us should have stayed in Philadelphia."

Claire looked at her, puzzled. "She's got Justin."

"Well, but poor Dad doesn't have anyone."

"Dad's in California," Claire reminded her. "And when he comes back, he's got Fluffy." Fluffy was Claire and Luna's brand-new stepmother. Her real name was Edith Hortense. Fluffy was just one of those terrible childhood nicknames that had stuck into adulthood.

Now Claire leaned forward and wagged a finger at Luna. "You don't really want to go to camp, do you, Luna? Crumbs, I knew it! You've got no zest for adventure!"

"Whatever!" Luna answered, but then she couldn't think of what else to say. She turned her head toward the window and listened to the conductor call the names of the stops that led all the way out to Bramblewine, the thirteenth stop, which was where their grandparents lived.

Maybe Claire was right. It was true that Luna did not like being caught by surprise. When she checked out a sad or scary book from the library, she read the last chapter first, just to be prepared. When she took a test, she made sure that she read the directions twice. When a spell called for a pinch, she measured out an eighth of a teaspoon. And she always, always liked her pencil to have a fresh eraser on one end and a sharp point on the other.

She liked to think of herself as careful. Cautious. Not zestless.

"Bramblewine!" shouted the conductor. As usual, Claire and Luna were the last two passengers left on the train. Nobody ever came all the way out to Bramblewine. In fact, most people did not even know there was a thirteenth stop. That's because Bramblewine was a rather mysterious place. And their grandmother, Five-Star Head Witch Arianna of Greater Bramblewine, was one of Bramble-wine's most mysterious residents.

"Hello, twinsicles!" Grandy called now, leaning out the window of her dusty old

Lincoln Continental. She was wearing her green-quartz-and-blue-topaz necklace and she'd had her hair beauty-parlorized, but her eyes looked a little squidgy.

"I'm still recovering from our Fourth of July party," she explained with a yawn as the twins climbed into the car. "We had almost a hundred people over. Your grandfather must have flipped two hundred soy burgers. You'll both have to sit in back, since Wilbur needs to stretch. Last night he swallowed a champagne cork, and he hasn't been himself since."

Wilbur was Grandy's cat, who often ate things he shouldn't. Grandy said the inside of his stomach probably looked like the bottom of the sea. Right now, Wilbur was asleep in the front passenger seat, snoring peacefully on his traveling cushion. He did not even twitch when Claire poked him.

"Hey, why weren't we invited to your party?" asked Claire.

"No kiddies allowed. Which reminds me, girls, how are your kittens?"

"They just had their shots," said Luna.

"Mom promised that she would take good care of them while we're gone."

"Mom says kittens are too much effort and she wishes you hadn't given them to us," said Claire. Luna elbowed her. Claire never knew when to keep her mouth shut.

Grandy did not seem to care. "A witch needs a cat," she said. "Your mother is not a witch, so she can't be expected to understand."

"Hey, Grandy, when did you know Mom wasn't a witch?" Luna asked.

"I knew the minute she was born, because she started to cry," said Grandy. "When a witch is born, she sneezes."

Claire, who (like Luna) was a one-star witch, faked a sneeze, and then fake-sneezed all the way to their grandparents' house. She was really getting on Luna's nerves today.

"She's just excited about camp," said Grandy, after Claire had jumped out of the car. Following the sound of Grampy's tractor, she sped down to the garden. "Claire has a love of adventure."

"*Zest*," mumbled Luna, shouldering

her bag. "You mean a *zest* for adventure."

Grandy raised her eyebrows. "Come upstairs and I'll show you something," she said. "Maybe it'll rub the doom off your gloom."

So Luna followed Grandy into the house and upstairs to the library.

The library was dark and smelled like books and spells and secrets. Glass-fronted cabinets stretched from the skin-thin antique Persian rugs to the high, water-stained ceiling. There was no air-conditioning at their grandparents' house, but the walls were so thick that the rooms stayed cool, even in July. Luna loved-loved-loved this library. It was her favorite room in any house, anywhere.

Grandy sat down at her desk chair and turned on a slim silver laptop computer that Luna had never seen before. "I recently downloaded my Big Book of Shadows," she said. "It's a lot easier for spell searches. Eighteen hundred pages take too long to thumb through, not to mention the mildew problems. Come here and sit by me."

Luna pulled up a chair. Grandy was quick on the keystrokes and did not have to look down at the letters once. She logged on and typed in "zest." Dozens of categories popped up.

```
Squeeze New Zest from
    Old Dandelions: Leaves
Squeeze New Zest from
    Old Dandelions: Roots
Take a Three-Minute Zest Test
Zesty Magical Herbs: Fennel,
    Flax, and Feverfew
Guatemalan Zesty Spiced Tacos
```

Carefully, Grandy scrolled down, and then highlighted the category marked Zest for Adventure. A long list of spells came up, but Grandy went right to the one called Marigold Zest.

"Aha," she said. "Presto perfecto." She double-clicked.

Luna read:

```
Marigold Zest:
A harmless adventure enhancement
Warning: do not confuse this
    spell with Marigold Pizzazz.
```

11

You will need:

Thrice-distilled marigold
    essence and clean feet

Directions:

Standing barefoot, facing west,

Three times chantyth, "Zest,
    zest, zest!"

Sprinkle powder toe to heel

'Twill soon provide that zesty
    feel.

Grandy clicked PRINT. "Since you are so good at memorizing, Luna, you should learn this by heart tonight," she warned. "It's a bad idea to take a written-down spell to camp, where it could fall into the wrong hands."

"Thanks, Grandy," said Luna, studying the paper. She did not quite know what the spell was about. Interesting, yes, but how could it help her?

"I'll be seventy-seven this year, but nobody can call Arianna Bramblewine a techno-turkey." Grandy patted her laptop and stood up. She crossed the room to unlock the door of one of her cabinets and took out a glass bottle of yellow powder. She blew the dust off its seal and held it up for Luna to see. "There you are, thrice-distilled Marigold Zest. This vial should *never* leave your care, though the smell is so unique it could be mistaken for some useless, overpriced cosmetic item. But a bottle of Marigold Zest can work wonders on even a non-witch's wishes. So hide it well! And if anyone asks you what it is, say it's homemade cornmeal foot powder."

She tossed the vial to Luna, who, after a moment's hesitation, slipped it into her pocket. "Thanks, Grandy."

"It'll put some temporary spring in your step," said Grandy.

Luna glumly rolled the bottle between her fingers. She would need more than a springy step to get through the next five weeks. Under Grandy's watchful eye, she felt her face grow warm.

"Grandy, I don't want to go to camp," Luna blurted. "And that's not the kind of thing that can be solved with spells. It's just my personality."

Grandy looked down her nose. "Nothing," said Grandy, "can be *solved* with a spell. Especially not the dinky one-star spells you and Claire are allowed to cast. But think how lucky you are, Luna. You're a twin! Imagine all the girls who brave camp alone."

"It's worse to be a twin! All camp will do is show how different Claire and I really are!" Luna wailed. "Claire's so much better for a place like camp. She can walk backward on her hands. She can whistle through her fingers. She never gets sun rash. I wish she hadn't talked me into stupid Camp Bliss. I wish I could stay here all summer and take care of the kittens!"

"Oh, they'll be fine. Cats are loners by nature. That's why they're such good pets. I'm more concerned about you." Grandy's brow furrowed. "Can you think of anything wonderful that might be at camp, that you wouldn't find at home or Bramblewine?"

Now it was Luna's turn to think hard. "Well, maybe one thing," she confessed in a voice slightly louder than a whisper. "I keep wondering if maybe my true, all-weather friend is at camp. Someone just for me."

"Well, there you have it!" Grandy thumped Luna's knee. "An all-weather friend is scarcer than finch-and-turtle soup. And I'd go farther than the Galápagos for finch-and-turtle soup. You're only going to Virginia."

2
Sailing to Bliss

WHAT CLAIRE REALLY WANTED to
know about Camp Bliss was: would there be a
tug-of-war?

"You always see tugs-of-war in the movies
and television shows about camp," she said,
leaning up to talk in Grandy's ear.

"Claire, sit back. Is your seat belt on?"
snapped her grandmother.

"Sometimes the tug happens over grass,"
Claire mused. "Other times there's a huge

mud puddle, and mud is what I'd rather—"

"You're blocking my rearview, Claire. Your belt's not on, is it?"

"—I'd rather tug over since I'm—"

"Sit back and buckle up, Claire!"

"—since I'm good at mud!"

They had been on the road since early morning, and now it was just past lunch. Luna was up front, with Wilbur on her lap. The reason Luna was up front, of course, was because she had started complaining that she was carsick from the moment she woke up that morning. Even before breakfast.

"How can you be carsick before you're *in* the car?" Claire asked.

"My anticipation that I will get carsick is almost as bad as the real thing," Luna answered primly.

Claire had a hunch that her sister only felt sick because she did not want to go to Camp Bliss. Even though Luna kept insisting it wasn't true, Claire's hunches usually were correct.

"If Camp Bliss doesn't have tugs-of-war, I'll enkindle one," Claire said. She had just learned the word *enkindle*. It was a fantastic word that made her think of a candle sparking into pale flame. Claire also had a hunch that *enkindle* was not working perfectly in her sentence, but it was hard to find the correct way to use a word like *enkindle* in regular, everyday talking. You had to grab your chances.

"If you don't sit back, Claire, I will enkindle your toes," said Grandy crossly. (Grandy was not using *enkindle* perfectly, either, but Claire decided not to say anything about that. Grandy was acting too crabby.)

"Besides," said Luna, turning around, "what does that mean, to be 'good at mud'? What do you think you are, a pig?"

Claire rolled her eyes, sat back, and refastened her seat belt. Grandy said it would take three more hours before they arrived at Bluefly, Virginia. Claire could hardly wait another minute. So far, it had been a pretty bad drive.

At first, Grandy had been enthusiastic about an all-day sight-seeing trip down south. "We'll do a quick detour through Roanoke.

That's where I met your grandfather, you know," she told them. "But first, we'll stop for a fish gumbo at this darling place I know in Baltimore."

But they got stuck in traffic and didn't find the darling fish gumbo place, after all. Instead, they had to eat a fast-food lunch. The take-out people forgot to make Grandy's drink diet. That's when Grandy started to grump.

"This trip was longer than I bargained for," she kept saying.

"A lot longer."

"It's never-ending. What was I thinking? Who the heck would ever want to go to Bluefly, Virginia? There aren't even any outlets."

Then Luna started getting grumpy, too, since grumpiness was in the air.

"Stop kicking the back of my seat," Luna complained. Or, once: "You didn't wash your hair last night, did you, Claire? I can smell it from up here. Yuck. It smells like dog breath."

And no matter what interesting subject

Claire brought up—did Camp Bliss have tugs-of-war? How much money would Justin make delivering groceries this summer? Would their kittens forget them after five weeks? What color did pink and green and a touch of mustard make? No matter what, it was nothing but crabbing from the front seat.

"Pink, green, and mustard is the color of carsick throw-up," said Luna.

"Pink, green, and mustard is the color of nondiet soda," said Grandy.

At one point, even old Wilbur looked up and yawned rudely in Claire's face.

So Claire was relieved, watching her grandmother in the rearview, when Grandy began to get her thoughtful, spell look. Grandy's spell face was unique among all others. First, she pressed her lips together so that they almost disappeared. Then her eyelids drooped. And then she started to nod her head. It all happened very, very slowly.

Claire crossed her fingers as Grandy cleared her throat.

"Girls," Grandy began, coaxing. "To get

this boring drive over with means casting a spell. I seem to have forgotten, however, the correct speed-driving spell. The only one that comes to my mind is a speed-sailing spell. But surely you do not want to sit in this car with me and my terrible mood for the next couple of hours, do you?" Her voice was loud and deep, ready to cast. "Young witches mine, be we in agreement? Aye or nay?"

"Aye!" shouted Claire.

"Aye," said Luna, very quietly because, Claire suspected, she did not want to get to Camp Bliss any earlier than she absolutely had to.

"Ayes have it. Hold tight!" Grandy ordered. With a tap of her finger north, south, west, and east on the odometer, she cast:

Batten down the hatches!
Blow, wind, blow.
We'll sail to Bliss
In the undertow.

There was a rush of freezing cold. Claire shut her eyes as what felt like a giant wave, then another, then a third, pounded and crashed the sides of the Lincoln Continental. It sounded so real and salty wet that Claire almost believed she was getting soaked. When she opened her eyes again, she realized that, as a matter of fact, she *was* soaked, and the car was pulling up between two blue-and-tan-striped pillars. Stretched between them was a canvas banner that read:

CAMP BLISS WELCOMES YOU!

"I'm drenched," squealed Luna. "Grandy, you splooshed us!"

"Eh, spell side effect. I should have told you to roll up your windows. But at least the car had a nice wash." Their grandmother turned on her windshield wipers and slowed over the speed bump. "Humph. Looks like we're right on time."

The parking lot was full. Dozens of girls milled around, waving to one another. Some carried tennis rackets. Some clung to their parents' hands. Some were wearing tan-and-blue-striped Camp Bliss T-shirts.

Claire scrunched down in her seat and tried to wring water from her shirt as she peered out the window. It was true, all of it! The rolling green fields, the curve of bright blue Lake Periwinkle in the distance, and even the posted wooden signs marked NATURE TRAIL or LODGE or SUPPLY HOUSE.

Just like in the pamphlet. Just like the camp of Claire's dreams.

Water squelched in her sneakers as she jumped out of the car. She hoped nobody noticed. Arriving at Camp Bliss all wet was not exactly the first impression Claire had wanted to give. She would just have to work with it.

The truth was that Claire wanted to be more than just another camper. She wanted to be the star camper! In fact, she wanted to be Camp Bliss Girl! She had read about it on the back page of the pamphlet. The counselors voted for the girl who "best embodied those characteristics of loyalty, sportsmanship, enter-prise, and bravery most exemplary of Camp Bliss." The winner received a two-handled sil-ver trophy. In the pamphlet, a picture showed last year's Camp Bliss Girl onstage, one shy hand held in Mrs. Carol the camp director's congratulatory grip, the other hand hefting her giant silver trophy.

"Loving cup" was what the pamphlet called the trophy. A perfect name for a big lovable hunk of silver!

Claire really-really-really wanted that loving cup. She had cleared a space on her bookshelf for it. She had already practiced her shy handshake.

She would be Camp Bliss Girl, and nobody was getting in her way!

Grandy parked in the lot, in front of the low white building marked OFFICE.

"Do you know any get-dry-quick spells?" asked Claire desperately.

Grandy rapped a finger against her temple. "Dry, dried . . . Well, I can make dried fruit from fresh, and I can cast a thirty-day drought anywhere in the tristate area, but actually, come to think of it, no. I don't know any spells for turning a wet person dry. Too bad."

As they walked up to the office, however, Claire saw Grandy quickly hop on one foot and mutter something to herself. When Claire looked at her again, Grandy was dry and pressed and perfect, as if she'd just spent a day at the beauty parlor.

"Hey! Grandy! You said you didn't—"

"Well, obviously I know how to attend to *myself*," said Grandy with a sniff. "Now, shush, because here comes somebody. Let me do the talking."

"Hi, there!" An older girl, dressed in white shorts and carrying a clipboard, came bounding down the steps leading from the office. She shook Grandy's hand politely. "My name is Pam Carol. I'm a senior counselor here. I'm also Jack and Brenda Carol's niece. They're the camp directors. You'll meet them later, at orientation." She glanced at the twins with dark eyes that matched her dark bobbed hair. "Are you the Bundkin twins?"

"My granddaughters," said Grandy. "I apologize that they're wet, but they were very hot and insisted on jumping in your lake for a quick dip. Do I need to sign any release forms, or may I leave now?"

"No, feel free to go, unless you want to stay for Uncle Jack and Aunt Brenda's tour. Your girls are ours."

Ugh! Claire did not like how Pam said "ours." Nor did she like how Pam handed over their two name tags without bothering to ask which name belonged to which twin.

"No, thanks! I hate tours. Besides, if you've seen one camp, you've seen them all." Grandy smacked a kiss on each twin's forehead. "Good-bye, dears. One of your parents will pick you up in five weeks, but I sure as heck won't be making this blasted trip again." She lowered her voice. "Good luck, and no unsupervised spells!" Then she jumped back into her gleaming car.

"How did you girls manage to get that car wet, too?" asked Pam as they all watched Grandy speed away.

Luna was silent, fiddling with her name tag.

"Um, we gave it a wash, since the lake was right there," Claire lied.

The smile dropped off Pam's face. "Okay,

listen up. I didn't want to be strict in front of your grandma and all, but here's the drill. First off, no washing of bodies or clothing or cars in Lake Periwinkle, nor is there any kind of jumping, splashing, or fooling around without permission from a senior counselor. Understood?"

She waited for the twins to nod yes. They nodded yes. It would be an easy rule to follow, since all witches hate-hate-hate still water. Lakes and witches have a bad history.

"Dandy." Pam checked her clipboard. "You two are in Cabin Four, Sleepy Hollow," she said. "That's my cabin. Cabin Three, Green Gables, belongs to my best friend, Tammy. She's also a senior counselor. We've been going to Camp Bliss since third grade. After Uncle Jack and Aunt Brenda, we pretty much rule this place. Me especially, since I'm their niece."

"How old are you?" asked Claire.

"Fifteen," said Pam. "Any other questions about my personal life? No? Dandy. Let's go."

Pretty rude, thought Claire. She looked

over at Luna, who stared glumly back. Luna was looking especially zestless today. Poor Luna. Claire would have to be a helping hand. Assisting the weaker campers was just the kind of good deed expected of a brave and enterprising Camp Bliss Girl!

They trailed Pam past the office and down a hill to where the cabins were arranged in a giant horseshoe shape. There were eight cabins in all. They were separated by age, Pam explained, so that eight-year-old "babies" bunked up in Cabin One's Sunnybrook Farm, all the way to "JCs" or junior counselors in Cabin Eight, Wuthering Heights. A senior counselor was assigned to each cabin, "to keep watch," Pam explained.

Which meant Pam would be sleeping in Sleepy Hollow, their cabin.

"*Yuck!*" mouthed Claire. Luna nodded, knowing what Claire's *yuck* meant. Pam was a rules-and-regulations counselor. She would not be much fun.

Both inside and out, Sleepy Hollow cabin was very plain. Like Abe Lincoln's house,

Claire thought. It had a big window facing out onto Lake Periwinkle, four wooden bunk beds, a cot (for Pam, Claire guessed), two sinks against the wall, and some scattered bureaus.

A few girls were sitting on their beds, drinking from juice cartons and chatting, while others were reclaiming their trunks. A radio was playing. It all seemed very cool.

Claire bounced a little in her wet sneakers. Camp!

Pam pointed out the window. "Those lean-tos are the showers and outhouses," she said. "There's one behind each cabin, so you'll have to work out timing. Hi, Tammy! What's up?"

Another teenaged girl, with a freckled tan and wearing the same counselor outfit as Pam's, had bounded into the cabin.

"No fair," she said, pointing. "You got the twins!"

"Big deal," said Pam. "They already took a dive into Lake Periwinkle. I've got my hands full of trouble, probably."

Tammy winked at Claire. "Well, I like trouble. I guess you girls will be our water-sports stars on Blue-and-Buff Day!"

"What's *buff?*" asked Claire, always on the alert for a new word.

"Um, it's our other camp color besides *blue?*" Pam answered in the same how-did-you-get-so-dumb? voice that Justin sometimes used. But Claire had known Justin all her life, and she had met Pam only five minutes ago. A how-did-you-get-so-dumb? voice was not a very friendly way to talk to an almost-stranger.

"Buff is another word for light brown or beige," said Tammy nicely. "Blue-and-Buff Day is our all-day sports competition. We pick captains, divide into teams, and compete for the title. Last year, the Blue Team won. That's why a blue flag flies over the camp. But I'm senior captain of the Buff Team, and I want a new flag raised! Check the back of your name tag. Is the sticker on it blue, or buff?"

Claire checked. "Buff!" she said. "Is there a tug-of-war?"

"Oh, yes! Plus rope climbing, canoeing,

archery, capture the flag, lemon-spoon balancing, volleyball, three-legged races—you name it. Okay, I better go round up my campers. See you later."

"Wait! Watch my trick!" Claire said. She wanted to impress Tammy quick before she disappeared back to the Green Gables cabin. But just as Claire dropped into a handstand (her plan was to walk backward on her hands), her foot kicked out into someone's leg, which, as she jumped right side up, she saw was attached to a skinny red-haired girl.

"Sorry," said Claire, although she had the feeling it was really the red-haired girl's fault.

The girl just rolled her eyes and brushed past.

"Show me later," called Tammy, with a wave good-bye.

Claire watched Tammy go with a heavy heart. Why did cool Tammy have to be a counselor for Green Gables, while she was stuck inside Sleepy Hollow with yuck, rule-crazy Pam?

And why did she have to be in the same

cabin as a mean red-haired girl who might have pushed against her and might have wrecked her handstand for totally no reason?

She looked over at Luna, who had found her trunk and was kneeling in front of it, unpacking and refolding and arranging her clothes carefully in the bottom drawers of a bureau. Luna was not going to be much help in this situation. She had not even checked her name tag to see if she was on the Blue or the Buff Team. (Claire checked—luckily, Luna's sticker was buff, too.)

If Claire wanted to be Camp Bliss Girl, well, she would have to figure it out on her own.

3

The Pillowcase Fund

LUNA DID NOT KNOW WHAT to do about her top-bunk sickness. As soon as she realized that there were no more bottom bunks left in the Sleepy Hollow cabin, the symptoms—a small cramp in her stomach and a drumming at her temples—started.

She tried to make the top-bunk sickness go away by thinking of nice things. Such as how peaceful her kitten looked when she slept in her basket. Or the taste of warm summer strawberries. Or the silken brush of beach sand between her toes.

All she could feel was sick at the prospect of sleeping in the top bunk.

She confessed her problem to Claire at that night's Welcome Campers cookout. Claire was no help.

"Toads and tamales, Luna! It's not my fault we got top bunks. Everyone called the bottom bunks before we came."

"I could sleep in the office. There's a first-aid room in the back. It has a bed. I saw it."

"Sure, go ahead. If you want kids to make fun of you, that is." Claire sniffed. "They'll call you names before camp has even officially started. Like Chicken Luna or Loser Luna or Luna Boo-hoo or—"

"Okay, okay. I get the point."

Luna could tell that Claire was distracted by so much else going on around them. So many new faces to see. So many names and rules and songs to learn. The last thing Claire ever would want to do was to sleep in the first-aid room and miss out on everything.

Zestlessly, Luna carried her paper plate over to a space all by herself and took a bite of her charred hamburger. She chewed and sighed and thought. Five weeks of teetering on the top bunk, and no way out. How long would she last? How would she even last the night?

After the cookout, there was a sing-along, and the counselors introduced themselves. Then the counselors performed a skit that tried to teach some of Camp Bliss's rules in a funny way. Then it was time for bed.

Camp is stupid, Luna thought, as she trudged back to Sleepy Hollow, where she changed into her nightshirt and brushed her teeth. And when it's not stupid, it's bad. Nothing but rules and burnt burgers and top bunks and smarty-pants Pam.

She went to the outhouse and stayed so long that girls yelled and pounded on the door for their turn. Just before she began the dreadful climb up, up, up to her top bunk, Luna thought about using her bottle of Marigold Zest, which she had hidden carefully in her bureau in her plastic soap case. But, no, zest was not what she needed. Zest would not help her get a good night's sleep on the top bunk.

Zest was not the same thing as bravery.

"'Night, guys," called Pam from her cot. "We're up at six tomorrow, so I'd advise against talking to your neighbors." She extinguished the door lantern. The cabin went dark and, after some giggles and whispers, quiet.

It was a terrifying first night. Every time Luna almost drifted off to sleep, she thought she could feel herself falling. Rolling down a mountaintop or plummeting through black outer space or dropping clean off the side of a—*argh!* She jolted awake with a start, her pulse pounding as her hands gripped the mattress edges. Safe! For now. Until she closed her eyes and was on the top of the mountain again. Oh, she would never get a good night's sleep!

A kick lifted her mattress from beneath.

"Would you shut up?" The voice was loud and deep, especially for a girl.

"Who's that?"

"It's me, Lakshmi, who sleeps under you. Or I'm trying to, at least. But it's pretty hard, with you muttering and groaning and sighing like some kind of haunted house."

"Sorry." Luna pictured Lakshmi's face, her velvet brown eyes staring up angrily at Luna's mattress.

"Get to know your cabin mates," Pam had told them earlier, at the cookout. "You're going to be spending a lot of time with them."

So Luna (who was good at memorizing) had matched up an adjective to the name of every girl who bunked in Sleepy Hollow. First came Know-It-All Pam, the counselor. Then Chunky Penelope. Then there was a red-haired girl, Ella, whom Claire had warned her was a jerk. (Jerk Ella, the red-haired girl.) Next was Nature-Girl Gladriole, or "Glad," who had waist-length bumpy hair and was a vegetarian. Then Laughing Min Suh, because she had a really loud, happy laugh that made everyone else crack up just to hear it. And Expensive Haley, who wore a ladylike gold watch and gold hoop earrings and had mentioned her vacation house in Bermuda three times already. And then there was Lakshmi, who was gorgeous, with perfect teeth and a silky black ponytail and even a little cleft in her chin. Luna was a big fan of clefts in people's chins.

Gorgeous Lakshmi.

Now Luna revised her list. Gorgeous Lakshmi, Who Hates Me.

Luna pushed herself closer to the wall. She squeezed her eyes shut. She was scared to be hissed at or kicked again. But just as she was about to fall asleep, she imagined that she was dropping off the side of the mountain, and (in spite of herself) she must have let out a very loud moan-mutter.

Below, Lakshmi gave a fed-up noise and muttered something herself. Something mean, Luna bet.

The next morning, Luna climbed down from her bunk, too humiliated to look at Lakshmi. She felt too shy even to apologize for keeping her awake. At breakfast, she watched out of the corner of her eye, ready to duck if Lakshmi decided to confront her. Which she probably would. Luna could sense that while Lakshmi was a quiet type, she was not meek. And while she kept to herself, Lakshmi didn't seem lonely. In fact, Lakshmi didn't seem to want to be at Camp Bliss at all.

Luna avoided Lakshmi until after breakfast. As soon as Claire got up from the table, Luna followed to sidle up behind her twin.

"You know that girl, Lakshmi? She hates me," she whispered.

"Lakshmi who?" Claire looked around.

"Lakshmi the Gorgeous Indian Girl. Don't look."

"Oh." Since Lakshmi was the only Indian girl at camp, Claire looked straight at her. Lakshmi stared straight back.

"Hi." Claire waved.

"Which one of you kept me up all night with your stomachache?" Lakshmi asked in her loud voice. "If you do it again tonight, I'm asking for a bed switch. No offense, but I need my sleep." She yawned.

"My sister has top-bunk sickness. She was scared to be up so high."

"I was dizzy. Not scared," Luna corrected.

"Oh." Lakshmi gave Luna a quick once-over, then turned her attention back to Claire.

"My sister's really good at drawing, though," Claire said. "She drew a picture of our kittens, and it was so cute."

"Uh, okay." Lakshmi shrugged.

"I'm Claire," Claire continued. "And if you really want to tell us apart, Luna's got a teensy little chicken-pox scar under her chin. See?"

Lakshmi squinted, then saw. "You shouldn't have scratched," she said.

How terrible, Luna thought, to have an ugly chicken-pox chin and be lectured to by a girl with a gorgeous cleft chin! She stared down at her feet and rubbed her finger over her scar and said nothing.

"Watch this," said Claire. She jumped out

of line, stretched into a handstand, and walked on her hands.

"Hey, that's pretty expert," said Lakshmi.

"You're from Los Angeles, right?" asked Claire when she came right side up again.

"Yeah," said Lakshmi. "I took a plane here. Five hours, all by myself." She clapped a hand to her mouth. "Oops! I've got to go to the office to call my dad and let him know I'm safe. I was supposed to do that yesterday."

"Put your tray on mine," said Claire, reaching for it. "I'll dump it for you."

Lakshmi handed over her tray. "Thanks! See you later."

Claire waved. "Bye." Lakshmi jogged off.

"See, Loon? She doesn't hate you." Claire smiled confidently. "The way I figure it, everyone would always rather be buddies."

Luna nodded. It was difficult to explain to her twin that she did not have Claire's same knack for making friends. Claire thought friends just appeared from nowhere on a sunny day and stuck naturally, like freckles.

After breakfast, the counselors and cabins

scattered for Early Meeting. That was when special announcements were made. Some counselors picked scenic spots by the tennis courts or Lake Periwinkle. Pam picked under a scrawny fir tree by the parking lot.

"Form a semicircle around me!" shouted Pam. Then she blew into her whistle. Of all the counselors, Pam seemed to be the most excited to use her whistle. She blasted it a lot.

Luna thought about sitting next to Lakshmi. Everyone would rather be buddies, she reminded herself. She sort of smiled at Lakshmi, who sort of smiled back. Chunky Penelope would be easier to sit next to, Luna thought. Penelope was so shy, and she looked like a girl who would be grateful for a buddy. Gorgeous Lakshmi would not be grateful. Luna could tell just by the way she was flopped at the edge of the grass, her ankles crossed, leaning back on her elbows and not noticing anybody.

Luna sat down next to Penelope.

"Hi," she said. Penelope smiled gratefully.

Pam blew into her whistle again. "Listen up, sports fans!" she said. "As you know, for the next five weeks, I run Sleepy Hollow. And this summer, as a senior counselor, I've decided to implement a new policy."

Luna gave Claire a thumbs-up, since *implement* was the word that Claire had won the fifth-grade spelling bee with this past spring. Claire was nuts about words. Claire gave a thumbs-up back.

"Twins!" shouted Pam, with a chirp on the whistle. "Please don't send each other cutesy hand signals while I'm talking. Understood?"

They nodded solemnly. Pam continued. "Here's my policy. We're going to pool our resources. That means each person has to donate to the Sleepy Hollow Cabin Fund. A certain something you brought from home that will be used by the whole cabin. Nothing big. I'm talking about a bottle of hand lotion, a sun visor, or maybe some homemade brownies your parents packed. Stuff like that. It's a great way for everyone to share! So check your trunks, your bags, or maybe even your pockets for something useful."

Pam unfolded a white pillowcase that she

had been carrying. "I'm leaving this pillowcase by the door of our cabin. Let's have nine donations in it by lunch. I'll go first." She took a pair of sunglasses from her pocket. "This is my spare pair, with UV-ray protection. For the next five weeks, anyone can use them." She dropped the sunglasses into the pillowcase. "Who's next?"

There was a silence.

Then a voice rang out, loud and stubborn. "No way."

The voice belonged to Lakshmi. Heads turned. Lakshmi brushed the grass from her hands. She was not smiling.

"Excuse me?" Pam fumbled at her whistle, although it was not exactly a whistle-blowing moment.

"I'm not donating to your pillowcase fund. All my stuff belongs to me."

There was a stirring of whispers. Luna let out a breath of relief. She didn't want to donate any of her things, either. She was a careful person, and she knew she had not packed anything for Camp Bliss that she wanted to share.

Pam smiled, but she looked annoyed. "Wow, Lakshmi, you're a party poop," she said in a falsely cheerful voice. "Anyone else want to be a party poop? Speak up, people!"

Silence.

Luna watched Pam, enjoying the look on her face, which was bright red and a touch scared. Maybe she was just starting to realize what a stupid idea this pillowcase fund was. Forcing people to share! As the silence lengthened, Luna bit her lip to hold back her smile.

"I have a box of saltwater taffy, and I hate saltwater taffy." Ella spoke up. "My mom put it in my trunk instead of my brother's by mistake." She shrugged. "I'll donate that."

"*Aaawwl* right! Now we're *talk*ing!" Pam whooped.

A couple of girls clapped.

"I've got a family-size tin of echinacea mints," said Claire. "They ward off respiratory diseases and they taste great, too!"

She said the last part in a goofy voice, and the girls laughed.

"I've got three bottles of sunscreen. My family always uses it when we go to our house in Bermuda," said Haley. "It's made with jojoba and hazelnut extract. It doesn't give you that greasy feel."

Luna looked over appreciatively. She hated-hated-hated her greasy sunscreen.

Penelope offered her radio with headset.

Min Suh donated the use of her special tennis racket, the same kind used by Venus Williams.

"I already have a way-nice tennis racket," said Haley. "How does that work for me?"

"It's a totally awesome donation!" said Pam. But Min Suh looked worried.

"What about my coconut shampoo?" she offered.

There was a show of hands. The tennis racket won over the shampoo.

Glad offered free foot massages.

"That's not really a donation," said Pam. "That's more like a service."

So Glad offered her fruit-leather snacks. "Made with no processed sugar and lots of love," she declared, and Luna got the feeling that everyone wanted the foot massages back.

Which left Luna and Lakshmi.

"Let me think about it," said Luna. "I can't figure it out right this second."

"Like I said, I'm donating nothing," said Lakshmi in her customary calm, loud voice.

"Then you're using nothing, okay?" Pam said. "It's not your fund if you don't contribute." Her face wore the relaxed, ear-to-ear grin of victory.

Lakshmi shrugged. She seemed completely unconcerned.

"Gosh, why does she have to be such a party poop?" murmured Penelope. Other girls looked over at Lakshmi reproachfully.

Lakshmi stood her ground. She did not seem to care a fig what people thought of her. Luna liked that, and she wished she had sat next to Lakshmi, after all. Then they would have been a team against Pam. A resistance.

After the meeting, when they were walking down to the field house to pick bikes for a morning ride, Luna screwed up her courage. She fell into step beside Lakshmi.

"I don't want to give anything to the Cabin Fund, either," she said.

"Luckily, it's optional," said Lakshmi.

"I feel really out of place here," Luna said, clearing her throat.

"Oh, yeah?"

"Don't you?"

Lakshmi stopped walking. "Why do you say that? Because I'm the only one here who's Indian American?" she asked. Not in a mean way, but her voice was loud.

"No, that's not what I meant," Luna said hastily. Her face felt hot.

"Then what *did* you mean?"

Luna had no idea what to answer. "I just meant . . . I don't know," she squeaked. "See ya later." She stumbled ahead, feeling stupid and hoping that Penelope would be around somewhere.

It was too horrible. Her one chance to be buddies, maybe even to make an all-weather friend, and she'd blown it.

4
Something's Brewing

"**A**ND ON THE SECOND NIGHT, Glad went upstairs to bed. As soon as she switched off her light, she heard it again . . . a *scritch-scratch-scritch*ing at the window."

Small smothered screams. Swallowed giggles. In the glowing firelight, the real Glad looked as if she might faint from fear. Claire knew she herself could not laugh. The whole trick of a great ghost story was to keep your eyes slightly zombied out and your voice a few octaves lower or higher than your own. As if some spirit were channeling this awful story through you.

"Who's there?" squeaked Penelope. "It's the one-eared pirate, right?"

"Shhh." Claire put a finger to her lips. "At first the scratch was very faint, but then louder. Again and again, it came . . . the sound of bony fingers *scraaap*ing against the glass." Through lowered lids, Claire sneaked a peek at the faces ringed around the campfire pit. Even Luna looked spellbound, and she'd heard the story, and the part about the *scraaap*ing, at least a hundred times. (Claire told it at every slumber party they'd ever attended.)

"*Scritch! Scratch! Scritch!*" Claire clawed the air with one hand. With her other hand, she snapped a twig between her fingers. A snap did not sound too much like a scritch or a scratch, but some of the younger girls jumped, then laughed.

"It was then, out of the darkest nowhere," Claire continued, "that a howling wind began to blow."

There could be no mistaking the sound of the low, howling wind that suddenly kicked up in the distance.

"Stop!" Penelope squeaked. "I'm too scared. Poor Gladriole!"

"It's not the real me," said the real Glad, twisting her hair. "It's just a story me."

Claire looked quizzically at Luna. Was she casting a spooky weather spell? But Luna shook her head. Claire raised her voice. "Glad sat up in her bed, terrified by the scratching and the wind. Had the ghost of old Wilbur, the one-eared pirate, returned?"

"I knew it!" Penelope squealed.

The wind shivered past, prickling scalps and scattering embers.

"Yipes!" exclaimed Tammy. "This weather! Maybe we should go in?"

Even Ella looked nervous.

"No, no! I'll finish quick," said Claire, half in her ghost voice, half in her Claire voice. "Glad ran to the window and opened it. Rain swept in, cold as a corpse and soft as tears."

When the sprinkle of cold rain began to

patter from the night sky, everyone started squealing.

"Who's doing that? Is this a prank?"

"Does someone have a watering can?"

"Shhh!" Claire pressed a finger to her lips and glanced angrily at Luna, who shook her head again. But of course it had to be her sister, Claire thought. Who else? Well, she wouldn't dare try anything for this next part. "Lightning flashed across the sky, turning the night bright as day. Gladriole could not believe what she saw, standing in the—"

White lightning jagged across the black sky. It was too much! Now came squealing and shrieking from the campers—and counselors—as they all jumped up from the campfire.

"There's cider and graham crackers at the lodge!" shouted Tammy. "Everyone, run. Ghost stories are over!" Quickly, she tamped down the little campfire with the flat end of a shovel.

Claire's story, the one she had been waiting all week to tell at the Saturday campfire, was ruined.

"You didn't need to send me all that extra-spooky weather!" she scolded as she came up behind Luna. "My ghost story was going great without your help. And Grandy would be mad at you for casting unsupervised spells."

"It wasn't me!" Luna turned, indignant. "You saw how I kept shaking my head no."

"Oh, yeah? Then who was it?"

"It must have been some strange coinci-dence," said Luna.

"Wind *and* rain *and* lightning? No way. Weather in threes is not a coincidence. I know a spell when I feel one, and so do you."

Luna shook her head. "I promise, it wasn't me," she said.

Claire was not convinced. "Hook on it?" She crooked her little finger.

"Sure," said Luna. After they hooked pinkies—because a pinkie hook is like crossing your heart, only twice as strong—Luna said, "Now that you know I didn't do it, Clairsie, I have tell you my sneaking suspicion. I don't think that weather was any coincidence." She linked her elbow through her sister's and bent her head to whisper. "Methinks there be another witch at Camp Bliss."

"Snakes and skullcaps! Here?" Claire cried; then, when Luna pinched her arm to pipe her down, she hissed, "How can you be sure?" Claire had never met another young witch—certainly not one in the eight-to-fourteen-year-old range. All the witches she and Luna knew were Grandy's friends. Old and cackling and opinionated.

"I've had my suspicions for a while. Only it wasn't till yesterday that I believed," Luna said, a bit mournfully. "See, my bottle of Marigold Zest has gone missing. Grandy gave it to me in case I needed zest. I memorized the spell and hid the bottle. Nobody but a witch could have sniffed it out. I'm so worried. Grandy super-extra warned me not to let it fall into the wrong hands."

"Are you sure Pam didn't take it and contribute it to the Pillowcase Fund?" asked Claire.

"I checked the pillowcase. I checked everywhere." Luna chewed her bottom lip. The theft had been weighing on her.

"We'll set a trap, then," Claire said. "We have a right to know who this mystery witch is! Especially if she's stealing our zest and wrecking our ghost stories."

"I've been doing some detectiving already," said Luna. "Whoever she is, she's got it out for Pam. Just watch how much Pam trips over her shoelaces. No matter how hard she ties them together, they keep coming loose. That's a silly, beginner-witch trick."

"But weather in threes is more advanced," Claire argued. "The Decree Keepers would be angry if they knew such a young witch was casting unassisted weather spells."

Luna shook her head. "I don't think this witch is paying attention to the Decree," she said. "She's casting so recklessly, like she doesn't care who catches her." She lowered her voice to a whisper again. "Methinks she be a rebel witch."

"Hard to believe there's a rebel witch at Camp Bliss," Claire said. "Everyone here is so normal."

"Well, we probably seem normal, too,

Clairsie," said Luna. "You'd have to wake up pretty early to catch us acting witchy. We never make mistakes like yawning with one eye open."

"Or twitching one nostril at a time."

"Or bending our toes backward."

"I haven't even cast one single food-seasoning spell," said Claire. "And all the meals here could use more oomph."

They were almost to the lodge.

"Keep your ears open and your eyes peeled," said Luna. "We need to find this rebel witch before she makes real trouble."

"I'll do better than just *find* her," said Claire, her hands curling into fists. "I'll catch her in the act."

She had to. A rebel witch was an official problem, Claire decided that night, as she lay awake on her top bunk. (Unlike Luna, she enjoyed sleeping up so high. The thinner air made her brain function more clearly, and she liked to touch the ceiling with her toes.) Why, a rebel witch could cast herself into the fastest runner! The scariest storyteller! The strongest tug-of-war puller!

A rebel witch, with no regard for the Decree, could even vote herself Camp Bliss Girl.

But to change Destiny, such as Claire's Destiny to be Camp Bliss Girl, could plop a witch into a vat of trouble. She could be boy-cotted. Fined. Her stars revoked.

"By hawthorn and the hay moon, ye shall be found, rebel witch," Claire muttered as she drifted off to sleep.

The next morning, every single one of the Sleepy Hollow girls looked suspicious to Claire. Suspect Number One was Ella, with her witch-red hair, who butted in lines and shoved at the sink and always used "Takes one to know one!" as her standard comeback.

Or Lakshmi, who talked loud as a judge and stalked around with her hands clasped behind her back, and who rebel-ishly said she would never give to the Pillowcase Fund.

Or maybe that girl, Glad, who was so dreamy and poetic. Poets and witches often overlapped.

Or even Min Suh, who laughed all the

way until it was time to pitch for the softball team, and then she turned into a tyrant, slamming knuckle and curveballs like nobody's business.

Yes, everyone had her witching moments. And those were just the girls in Sleepy Hollow.

It was too much to think about. And soon, Claire forgot to think about it. Especially after the next morning's nature walk, when she was the first to spot a purple speckled blue jay, the official bird mascot of Camp Bliss. Later that afternoon, she did twelve chin-ups at the "test-your-fitness" obstacle course, making her the chin-up champ in her age division.

It was, all in all, a great day. By dinnertime, Claire decided that even if there was a rebel witch at Camp Bliss, she wasn't anyone to lose sleep over. No, this mystery witch was not aiming to sneak off with Claire's loving cup. She was probably just a wee witch, a Cabin One girl who didn't know any better.

By the next morning, Claire had pretty

much put the whole thing out of her mind when two incidents made her think again.

First, she saw Pam trip.

Ever since Luna mentioned that the rebel witch held a grudge against Pam, Claire had been keeping an eye peeled, waiting to see when Pam might stumble next. While there had been a million great opportunities to trip her up—especially during yesterday's softball game—Pam stayed standing.

Luna was imagining things, Claire had decided after the softball game.

It wasn't until the next morning, while she was checking names for roll call, that Pam suddenly and inexplicably tripped and fell. Hard.

"Ow! Dang!" Pam staggered to her feet. "It's like my knees keep giving out!"

Which was precisely how the spell worked! A tap on each knee and a quick:

Knock these knees—
Fall to thine!

The spell was in the Baby Book of Shadows; that's how simple it was.

From the way Pam was rubbing her dusty knees, it also looked pretty painful. Claire glanced around. The Green Gables girls and Cabin Five's Plum Creek girls were lined up for roll call. Just beyond, a group of junior and senior counselors were lounging in and around the oak-tree hammock.

Claire looked down the roll-call line at Luna, whose face was pinched in worry. She had seen Pam fall, too, and had heard her remark. Claire knew that Luna was thinking the same thing: Yes, Pam was annoying; but, no, she sure did not deserve being cast around and tripped up by some mean rebel witch.

Claire literally stumbled on the next clue a couple of hours later, after dinner. Tammy had invited her on a twilight walk along with the Green Gables cabin, and Claire was trotting over to Green Gables, scouting for fireflies, when she saw a lump of freshly turned grass.

She was about to stomp it down with her foot when she caught the thinnest whiff of apple. Claire's nose was exceptionally good. She could pick out the faintest, most scentless odors, such as feathers, saltine crackers, or sand.

She followed her nose to where the smell was its strongest, then quickly crouched and dug and dug until she was holding a quarter-section of a green Granny Smith apple.

Claire knew she had stumbled upon evidence of a spell. More important, it was evidence of a problem-solving spell. Here's how the spell worked:

> *Tell your problem to the apple, then*
> *polish and quarter it.*
> *Whisper four possible solutions into each*
> *of the four sections.*
> *Bury the sections North, South, East,*
> *and West.*
> *After a week, dig all the sections up.*
> *Whichever section of the apple is least*
> *rotten is the best solution to the*
> *problem.*

But anyone knows that is a very quaint and bygone way to solve a problem. An Old School spell, Claire thought irritably. With about twenty-five percent accuracy. No modern witch wasted her time whispering to apples and digging them up. Whoever was teaching this rebel witch was using a very out-of-date textbook.

Angrily, Claire dug up the remaining sections and tossed them high into the trees. Of all the camps to pick, she thought, why did some strange Old School rebel witch have to come sneaking into her very own Camp Bliss?

"I'm onto ye, trouble-enkindling Old School rebel witch," Claire said out loud, in case the rebel witch was somewhere out there. Spying on her.

Which was a pretty spooky sensation.

5
Luna Boo-hoo

ONE AND A HALF WEEKS down, Luna thought. Three and a half to go. She tried to remember what three and a half weeks in the past had felt like. She counted back to late June and the last day of school, when their fifth-grade teachers, Mrs. Fleegerman and Mr. Rosenthal, had taken them out to Wild Water Park for an end-of-the-year school trip. There had been a fun house and an observatory and a homemade fudge stand. Luna and Claire had shared a bag of white-chocolate fudge with pineapple chunks. Delicious!

The taste of pineapples and chocolate seemed like a million years ago.

It would be impossible to stay at Camp Bliss for three and a half more weeks, Luna decided. What was the point? She had not made an all-weather friend, though she was friendly with a lot of girls. Especially Penelope. That was mostly because they both were picked last for teams.

And every time she climbed all the way up to the top bunk, she was sure this was the night she would fall and break her arm.

In fact, the only place where she felt comfortable was the first-aid office. Probably since she'd spent so much time there.

It wasn't her fault. Bad things kept happening to her.

For example, in spite of applying plenty of Haley's fancy sunscreen, Luna came down with a skin-splotching rash. "Sun poisoning," Pam said. "Go see Talita in the office. You're excused from afternoon sports."

Luna went down to the office to find Talita, who used to go to Camp Bliss but now was in medical school. Now, as a summer job, she was in charge of all the Camp Bliss paperwork, plus head of first aid.

Talita gave Luna some calamine lotion and a paperback to read while she recovered in the first-aid bed. The paperback was called *Eternally Eustacia*. It was an old-fashioned romance with lots of good descriptions of ball gowns and horseback riding.

When the rash faded into little pink bumps, Luna thought she was getting better. By the next morning, the bumps had started to itch. It turned out she had a case of poison sumac.

"Okay, Luna, you are excused from the basketball tournament," said Pam with a frown.

Luna trotted to the first-aid office, where Talita mixed up a baking powder paste to stop the itch. She took another rest on the first-aid bed and read a couple more chapters of *Eternally Eustacia*. Then she and Talita played crazy eights.

"It's fun to get a break from solitaire," Talita said.

Luna smiled. Talita was nice. She had shiny eyes, and she wore her hair in little braid circlets she called twisty-ties. She promised she'd twisty-tie Luna's hair one day when she had the spare time.

The poison sumac was almost gone the next morning when Luna woke up with a bloody nose. "We're in a mountainous region," Talita explained when she was summoned from the office to Luna's bunk side. "Don't be scared. It's natural. Keep pinching your nose at the bridge."

The nosebleed cleared up, but the next day Luna was back in the first-aid office because she had stepped into a thicket of nettles. Talita had to use tweezers to pick them all out.

"If there was a blue ribbon for being accident-prone, you'd get it," Talita said as she swabbed Luna's ankles with disinfectant. "All set."

"How about a hand of crazy eights?" Luna

looked around the first-aid room with longing. It reminded her of a combination of her mother's examining room and Grandy's library. A good balance of dark wooden beams and sterilized instruments.

"Okay," said Talita. "And then you need to get back to camp."

But after crazy eights, they played go fish, and then one of the campers, Janna Bruskaard, came in with a scraped elbow. "I hope I'll be healed by the canoe trip tomorrow," she said. "Everyone says I'm a star paddler!"

"Don't worry about a thing," Talita comforted her. Then Luna watched as Talita swabbed, sprayed, and bandaged Janna's elbow and told her how brave she was. Talita will make a good doctor, Luna thought. She was calm and decisive.

Talita was teaching Luna rummy five hundred and telling her about her boyfriend, Curtis, when the dinner bell rang.

"Gosh, that's the first time the bell took me by surprise!" Talita said with a laugh. "You go ahead. I've got to finish up some paperwork here. Guess I took a little bit of a sick day myself."

"See you later," said Luna.

"Or sooner." Talita waved.

Sooner or later turned out to be the next morning. Right after breakfast, Luna felt a touch nauseated. Instead of canoeing over to the bluffs along with the rest of her cabin, she decided she had better rest up until her stomachache passed.

"Yeah, yeah, yeah," said Pam when Luna approached her. "Go see Talita."

"There's nothing I can do about indigestion except give you some Peptine," said Talita.

"Can I can help you with stuff around here, until I feel better?" Luna asked.

"Act-u-a-lee," said Talita, pulling on every syllable as she looked at Luna, "there is something. See that brown box? We got some new supplies in, and I haven't had a minute to unload them. But you're canoeing today, right? You don't want to miss something as fun as that."

"I don't mind," said Luna truthfully.

She spent the rest of the day unloading the carton of supplies, and then taking inventory for Talita. In the cool quiet indoors, Luna counted and checked cotton balls, Q-tips, gauze bandages, and disposable thermometer strips. After she finished, she watched Talita update the Camp Bliss Web page.

That's when Luna had an idea.

"May I write a letter home on behalf of the campers?" she asked. "It might add a nice personal touch."

"Be my guest," said Talita. "I never think anyone reads this Web page, anyhow."

Luna jumped on the computer.

It's been two weeks and we are having more fun than we ever dreamed! The sun shines all day long, and the nights are filled with campfire song! she typed. Today a bunch of us went canoeing. Everyone considers Janna Bruskaard to be one of the star paddlers.

"Nice. You could do daily updates and call it 'Luna's News,'" said Talita, looking over her shoulder. "It would be great, especially for the parents of the younger girls, the kiddies who haven't been away from home before."

"Okay," Luna agreed. Perhaps writing cheerful bulletins about Camp Bliss would convince her that it was a fun place to be.

The next day, the entire camp was going to ride bikes along the Bluefly Ridge trail.

"So get psyched!" yelled Tammy and Pam. The girls whistled and stomped. Luna cringed. She checked for nosebleed, rashes, fever. Nothing. During cabin cleanup, she even hung her head off the side of her bunk bed, but not so much as a trickle of top-bunk sickness ran through her. She felt great!

That meant it was time for her last-resort tactic. A spell. It wasn't a big-deal spell. It was more like a trick, one she had seen Grandy do for her friends at parties, with a wineglass balanced on her head. Luna guessed that the wineglass part was unnecessary.

Quickly, she said her name frontward and backward, then touched her forehead and tongue and cast:

There once was a girl who was weller
So she decided to cast her own speller.
She made her skin cold

Filled her mouth up with mold
From the sickly you now couldn't tell her.

Then she ran down the hill and straight to the front office. The spell was so mild it would wear off in twenty minutes. She had to be quick.

"Good gracious!" Talita put her hand over her heart. "Your tongue is green and fuzzy." She placed a palm on Luna's forehead. "You're cold as an ice cube! I don't know what to do for that. I've never seen anything like it before, not even in my textbooks." She looked so concerned that Luna felt bad.

"It doesn't hurt at all, really," she said. "I'm sure I'm fine."

"Hmm. I should keep a close watch on you for a while." Talita held up her pack of playing cards. "Want to play? That is, if you're up to it?"

"Sure!" Luna smiled.

At lunch, they split a cream-cheese-and-olive sandwich, and then Talita had to go teach a water-safety session to the Cabin One and Two girls. "We need to keep reminding the little rascals, otherwise they get too bold," Talita explained. "You can stay here and answer the phone while I'm gone."

"Okay!" Luna was pleased to sit at the front desk. It had a computer and a big stack of Talita's medical textbooks. This is what it would be like to be in college or have a job, she thought. With no more camp, ever.

She took *Eternally Eustacia* out of the desk top drawer. She was almost to the end of the book, and she was sure that a beautiful wedding would be coming up in the last chapter. Talita had said that when Luna was finished, she could donate it to the Pillowcase Fund.

After a few minutes, she was interrupted by a loud screaming from outside. "Help me, Taleeetaaa! I'm going to die!"

Luna looked out the window. Haley was hopping over the hill, holding her toe with both hands and crying at the top of her lungs. Luna hurried out and helped her into the office, and then helped her onto the first-aid cot.

"What seems to be the trouble?" she asked in her best doctor voice.

"There's a gargantuan splinter in my toe! I got it on the dock!"

Luna looked. Sure enough, the half-inch splinter lay buried like a crooked frown under the thick skin of Haley's big toe.

"Do something!" Haley moaned.

"We should wait for Talita," said Luna.

"But I might get an infection!" Haley bawled. "If you stand by and do nothing, then you could go to jail. My parents are lawyers, so I should know!" Tears squirted from her eyes like watermelon seeds.

Although Luna didn't quite believe this threat, her heart raced. Talita would not be back for at least half an hour, and Haley's crying was already unbearable. Luna examined the toe more thoroughly. Simple, really. Nothing to it. Sterilize a pair of long tweezers, some rubbing alcohol . . .

"Okay, I'll do it," she said, "but you have to stop crying."

"I can't!" Haley cried. "I'm in more pain than I ever felt in my life!"

Luna doubted this was true, but she briskly

washed her hands in the basin and selected the tweezers and alcohol from the first-aid cabinet. "Don't wriggle," she instructed. "Please, Haley. If you cooperate, this will be over in no time."

"Hurry! The splinter is poisoning my blood as we speak!" screamed Haley. "I might have to get an amputation!"

"Oh, that's ridiculous! You need to sit still, so that I can do my job," Luna exclaimed. Haley's crying was rattling her nerves. Maybe they should wait for Talita, after all.

"The splinter is touching my toe bone!" Haley screamed.

"Please, Haley, keep still," Luna begged. But Haley was not going to stop wriggling or screaming.

Then Luna remembered that Talita kept a glass jar of sour balls in the lower cabinet. She grabbed Talita's keys from the desk, unlocked the cabinet, reached in, and selected a green one.

"I'm not a baby!" wailed Haley. "I don't need candy!"

"No, this isn't candy. This is a medicine ball.

It helps the pain," said Luna. "It has a special . . . potion. Only the green ones, though. That's why they don't taste quite as good as the others."

Haley looked skeptical, but she grabbed the candy and unwrapped it. As she slurped on the sour ball, the tears dried on her cheek. Luna took a deep breath as she again sat on the stool opposite the first-aid cot. She kept a firm grip on Haley's toe and slowly, painstakingly, drew out the splinter.

"*Voilà!*" She held up the splinter for Haley's red-rimmed eyes.

"Wow!" Haley sniffled. "It didn't even hurt much. That's strong medicine."

"What's going on here?"

Luna turned. Talita was standing in the doorway, her arms crossed and eyebrows raised.

"She saved me from a splinter." Haley wriggled her bandaged toe. "See that? Luna did as good a job as a real doctor."

"It was nothing," said Luna, embarrassed.

Later, after Haley left, Luna told Talita the

whole story. Talita laughed. "Green sour balls. I'll have to remember that!" she said. "Good work, Luna."

That evening, Talita must have said something to Pam, because straight after dinner, Pam walked up to Luna and dropped a hand on her shoulder.

"Luna, congratulations on your first-aid work. Talita says you're a good apprentice."

"Um, if you really feel that way," Luna began nervously. "The truth is, I'd rather be up in the front office, helping out and working on the Web page. I like doing that better than regular camp stuff."

"Yeah, yeah, yeah," said Pam. "I've been thinking about you, Luna. I have a proposition." She drew Luna a little way apart from the rest of the girls to speak privately. "I don't want this getting out since it's not really Camp Bliss policy, but here is my idea. If you put in more effort and enthusiasm during the morning camp activities, then I'll let you off for afternoon office duty. Talita said she could use the help, and if you're participating with us in the

morning, then I don't have a problem with it."
She stuck out her hand. "Team player?"

Luna stuck out her hand, too. "Team player!"

"Dandy." They shook on it, and Pam blew on her whistle, which seemed like the right thing to do after a deal had been struck.

6

Calling Camp Bliss Girl

ELLA WAS THE REBEL witch. Claire
could feel it in her bones. She could sense it in
her skin. She could smell it in the air.

"Oh, don't be so dramatic," said Luna,
peering down from her perch on the dock.
"Come out of the water. I'm getting dizzy just
looking at you. Don't you feel dizzy?"

"Nuh-uh, it doesn't bother me anymore. I
love-love-love Lake Periwinkle!" To prove it,
Claire spun herself around in her inner tube.

This made her horribly dizzy. But a real Camp Bliss Girl should not be scared of water!

"Besides," Luna continued, "what do you have to go on, besides your dramatic hunches?"

Claire gritted her teeth. It was hard to explain. "Ella Edsel's a cootie-faced Jerk from Berserk," she said.

"So is Angelica Antonio," Luna reminded her. "She's the snootiest girl in the whole school, remember? But we never thought Angelica was a rebel witch. Actually, I'm surprised you don't get along with Ella. You're both good at all the same things."

"Never, ever, lump me with Ella Edsel," said Claire sternly. "She is rotten. She is wrecking my chances to win the you-know-what." Claire never liked to say those wonderful words "loving cup" out loud. It seemed like a jinx.

"She might be rotten, but she's not a rebel witch," said Luna.

Claire stretched out her arms and recited:
"From A to zed and here to there,
In buckled shoes and wild red hair,
With warted chin and toothless smile,

Shalt spy a witch from o'er a mile."

Luna snorted back a laugh. "That's from our nursery school book of spooky poems, Clairsie! You might as well hunt down Ella's broomstick and cauldron, if your hunches are going to be that old-fashioned."

"There's a grain of truth in every poem," said Claire haughtily. "And you have to admit, Loon. Her hair is *wild* red. Besides, you don't watch Ella Edsel the way I watch Ella Edsel."

On that point, Claire was certain. Nobody at Camp Bliss was watching Ella Edsel as carefully as Claire Bundkin.

That was because, in addition to being (probably) the rebel witch of Camp Bliss, Ella Edsel was a *saboteur*.

"Saboteur!" Claire would mutter under her breath whenever she saw Ella loping along on her spider-skinny legs. Claire was very happy she had learned that word. It meant someone who wrecks another person's plans, and it fit Ella perfectly (better than *traitor*, which was too soldierly, or *weasel*, which sounded almost cute, like a pet).

Ella Edsel's name even sounded saboteur-ish, with that stylish double E. For the first time, Claire was glad she wasn't a triple-B name, like Bonnie-Blue (her favorite name in the entire world).

"Bonnie-Blue Bundkin is *not* a stylish name! It's vile. It sounds like a bunny rabbit," her mother had insisted. "You'll thank me later, Claire."

Ella Edsel is also a vile name, Claire thought, because it's attached to a vile person. A pusher and a kicker and a cheater and a two-faced *saboteur*. If Ella Edsel was also a rebel witch, that was just one more thing to add to a long list of bad qualities.

It was frustrating to Claire that Luna never saw how bad Ella was. In fact, most everyone missed it. For some reason, girls liked Ella. They never appeared to notice her non-stop cheating. Such as how she would call, "Safe!" when she was really out, or how she didn't quite show people her time on the stop-watch, and how she always took do-overs for archery and gymnastics.

Once, during afternoon pottery, Claire saw Ella's vase collapse on the wheel. After Pam redid it, Ella took full credit for Pam's work.

"Mine turned out great," she bragged into Claire's ear. "Mine's the best!"

"Um, I think you mean *Pam's* is the best?" Claire sneered.

"She only helped me for a sec," said Ella. "Jealous, much?"

"Cheater, much?"

Ella just batted her eyes and skipped away to place her vase in the kiln.

It would have taken nothing to cast a "puff-o'-the-wind" spell. One unexpected breeze to smash that vase to bazillion pieces. If only Grandy hadn't said No Spells! Well, it was probably for the best. Claire didn't need anyone to think she was a bad sport. Bad sportsmanship was not part of the Camp Bliss Girl identity.

Ella knew that, too. She had also figured that she and Claire were neck and neck for the silver loving cup, even though Claire had played dumb about the whole thing.

"Takes more than beginner's luck to be C. B. G.," Ella said after their first competition. They had tied for the win in the junior wind-surfing race. She stood over Claire after she had collapsed on the bank, woozy from too much time on Lake Periwinkle.

"What's C. B. G.?" Claire wheezed.

"Oh, like you don't know, Flea!" Ella scoffed. "Camp Bliss Girl, obviously. It's the best camper award. Julianna Becker won it last year! This year she's not here because she's working as a lifeguard in Newark, New Jersey. She taught me everything I know. And you might as well give it up and settle for second-place ribbons. The trophy never goes to a rookie camper. Like you."

"I'd rather be a rookie camper than a cootie monster."

"Listen, for the last time, I don't have cooties!" Ella stamped her foot. "Stop telling people that!"

"Cootie germs, no returns," Claire answered, sitting up to punch Ella's ankle with the last of her strength. On the inside, her hopes felt as crunched as an old tin can.

Was it true? Could a loving cup only go to a returning camper?

No way!

Ella Edsel was also a liar, Claire reminded herself. A liar who was feeling the heat of competition.

Because it was always Claire or Ella. Ella or Claire.

At any game or relay, at any sailing or swimming race, at any fitness test, and even at any contest that girls made up for fun—such as who could long-jump farthest off the top of the stone barbecue grill, or who could eat a slice of pizza in the fewest bites—Ella and Claire finished too close for comfort.

Sometimes Claire won. Sometimes Ella won. Sometimes they tied.

And mostly, Claire decided, Ella cheated.

When Ella's cheating was too obvious, Claire had to speak up. "But Ella didn't touch the buoy!" "Ella added ten points to her scorecard!" "Ella netted the ball twice and didn't call it!"

"You're nuts!" Ella yelled. "You're blind!"

In such a loud voice that Pam would let her off. Probably, Claire figured, because it was easier to allow Ella to get her way than to question her.

So Claire had to be content with whispering. "Cheater!" "Liar!" "Jerk!" "Saboteur!"

"Takes one to know one!" Ella always whispered back.

Which made Claire grit and grind her teeth. How long could she keep being a good sport without going crazy?

The last straw was the afternoon mountain hike for advanced hikers only. Midway up to Bluefly Ridge, Ella jumped directly ahead of Claire. Then, while pretending to clear the path, she snapped back some pricker branches so that they scratched Claire's arm.

"Ow!" Claire yelled, extra loud.

"Sorry, Fleabite," said Ella in a singsong voice. Then she muttered a few words under her breath.

Claire gasped. Was it a spell? A rebel-witch pricker-stinging spell? It had to be! Proof, at last!

Suddenly, the prickers seemed to sting more fiercely. After they descended the mountain, Claire raced to the first-aid office, where Talita and Luna cleaned and dressed her arm.

"What did I tell you!" Claire exclaimed once Talita was out of earshot. "Rebel-witch Ella Edsel snapped the pricker branch on purpose! Then she chanted a spell to make it sting worse! It feels like fire on my arm!"

"Really? A pricker-sting spell? How'd it go?"

"Well, I didn't hear it, exactly."

"Could it have only been your imagination?"

When Claire didn't answer, Luna looked skeptical. "Careful, Clairsie," she warned. "Whatever Ella did or didn't do, you don't want to come off looking like the baddie."

"*She* hurt *me*! How'm I the baddie?"

"Well . . . the way you tell those jokes at dinner, saying Ella has cooties. Or how you say that she has lice, and that her lice probably have red hair and freckles, too."

"Oh, that's just camp spirit! Haven't you ever heard her call me Flea or Fleabite? Ella Edsel's like a—a human pricker! I wish I could figure out the best spell to get her back."

"Ignore her."

Claire wrinkled her nose. "You sound like Mom and Dad."

"Rise above it."

"Luna! That's not real advice."

"And whatever you do, don't sink to her level."

Claire snapped her fingers. Aha! She would sink to Ella's level. She would pretend to be friends, and then when nobody was looking—*bam!* Right back at her. "Thanks, Loon! Great advice!" she said, giving her sister a hug.

She bided her time and waited for the perfect opportunity. It would be just a one-time warning, she decided. To show that two could play saboteur, ha ha! She practiced jabbing her finger right in Ella's face and saying, "How's that for a taste of your own medicine, cootie monster?"

The golden moment came during an

afternoon pickup soccer match out in Cow Patty Pasture. Soccer was one of Claire's favorite sports. It got a lot of her running energy out. She liked to play offense, but usually she had enough steam in her to play defense, too. Basically, she just followed the ball wherever it went.

Ella had extra running energy, too. She played by Claire's same rules of following the ball all over the field, only more aggressively. Her usual trick was to swipe the ball to the extreme sideline, so that it was almost out of bounds. That's when she would drive it all the way down the field, yelling, "I got it! I got it!" so loud that nobody else came near her.

Usually, Claire stayed out of Ella's way, too. Safe from her bumps and shoves.

This time, she was ready. As soon as Ella got the ball, Claire streaked up alongside, tapped her knees, and softly chanted:

Knock these knees—
Fall to thine!

Immediately, Ella stumbled and fell flat as a skinny squished spider.

In the next instant, Claire had recovered

the ball. She pointed her finger and began, "How's that for a taste of your own—" but already Ella had bounced back up, so Claire had to pass the ball, quick. Which she did, to Zoë, who popped it to Janna, who smashed it past Penelope and into the goal.

Everyone cheered. Ella scowled.

Ella pointed at Claire indignantly. "She tripped me!" she yelled to Pam.

"How did I?" Claire bellowed back.

"You said bad words to me, Fleabite!" Ella shouted. "You used intimidation tactics!"

Pam narrowed her eyes, called a time-out, and trotted over from the sidelines. "Keep it down, girls; they can hear you in Kentucky. That doesn't sound like you, Claire. Did you say anything intimidating?"

"Crumbs, of course not!" said Claire. She made herself look Pam in the eye. "*I* never cheat."

Lying was weird. Kind of like telling a campfire ghost story, as if the zombie version of Claire were channeling bad words through her real self.

Pam looked from Ella to Claire and back again. She seemed to be trying to decide something. "No penalties," she called finally, blowing her whistle.

As soon as Pam's back was turned, Claire stuck out her tongue. Ella mouthed a curse word. Claire mouthed a worse curse word back. Ella yawned and tapped her hand over her mouth, then scooted off before Claire could do anything more.

Uneasily, Claire waited for Ella to cast her knock-these-knees spell, or worse, but nothing happened.

Ella's team evened the score, ending the game in a tie. But a spell-cheat tie, Claire realized, did not feel the same as a real one.

After everyone shook hands down the line, Pam signaled for Claire and Ella both to come stand on either side of her. She flung an arm around each of their necks and drew them into a three-way huddle.

"Look here, sports fans. Healthy competition is part of Camp Bliss's identity, but in the end, we're all on the same team, Team Bliss," she said. "So you girls better call a truce."

Ella smiled. "I'm real sorry, Claire," she said in a sticky voice. "Maybe I was hearing things. I'm sure you didn't make me trip on purpose. Truce!"

Claire swallowed. How could Ella be so two-faced? Why couldn't Pam see how fake Ella really was?

"Okay, I'm sorry, too," she said. "Truce."

"Dandy." Pam blew on her whistle. "Now let's go eat. It's corn dogs and three-bean salad tonight. Hup two."

"Yee-haw!" Ella leaped and sprinted away to catch up with the rest of the team.

Truce *for now*, Claire thought sourly as she straggled alone up the field.

She had a feeling that, like most truces, it was waiting for the right time to be broken.

7

An Extra Kick

LUNA NOTICED that the rebel witch was changing the food.

The tacos became crunchier. Fresh oregano flecked the spaghetti sauce. The stale lemon squares now tasted lemony and didn't crumble to dust.

Soon, everyone else noticed. The counselors were mystified. They discussed it endlessly. "Maybe the chef from Camp Haligalouk has become friends with Chef Sue," Tammy said. Camp Haligalouk was the boys' camp. It was way over on the other side of Lake Periwinkle. Sometimes the girls would see one of the boys' maroon-painted boats on the lake or smell the smoke from their grill, but for the most part, the camps did not bother with each other. Besides, Sue, the Camp Bliss chef, was rather short-tempered. It did not seem likely that she would make friends or trade her recipes.

Other girls guessed it was a ghost.

Luna did not have to guess. She knew. The improved lemon squares were a dead giveaway. They had a perfect, no-mistakes taste. A witch's work, without a doubt.

"At least the rebel witch is not tripping Pam anymore," Luna remarked after a delicious dinner of savory vegetarian chili.

"That's because the rebel witch is Ella Edsel, and she's got it out for *me*, not Pam," said Claire. She burped and blew it in Ella's direction.

Luna shook her head. She was sure the rebel witch was not Ella Edsel. For one thing,

Ella did not care about food. Luna knew this, because once she saw Ella eat one of Gladriole's fruit leathers out of the Pillowcase Fund. Nobody could stomach those fruit leathers. They tasted like honey-coated tires.

Before the mystery could be solved, the food returned to its same bad taste. Again, the spaghetti sauce was runny as tomato juice. Again, the tacos sogged. The lemon squares turned back to dust-crusted bricks.

"I guess Chef Sue lost interest," said Tammy sadly.

"I guess rebel Ella is sick of cooking spells," Claire confided to a doubtful Luna.

It wasn't long, though, before the rebel-witch struck again. This time, the spells were odd in a completely different way. For the next couple of days, Camp Bliss seemed extra blissful. The counselors started wearing wisteria and ivy flower wreaths. Nighttime story hour began to stretch late into the night. It seemed as if everyone had a poem or a song or a feeling to share.

"This is the greatest, most beautiful group

of campers, ever!" Pam rasped one evening, her voice hoarse from so much singing. "There is such peace in the air! Come on, girls, let's sing another round of 'Hawaiian Rainbows'!"

"It's like the rebel witch cast some sort of sappy-feelings spell," said Claire. "Yuck."

Privately, Luna was glad that the rebel witch had decided to use her powers on nice food and sappy feelings. It was better than tripping Pam or casting wild weather.

Soon the flowers and songs stopped, too. Everything went back to normal. Unfortunately, Luna sensed danger in the air. The danger of a thing about to happen, she thought.

All week during her office duty, she tried to phone Grandy. First to confess about the long-lost Marigold Zest, and then to ask what to do about the rebel witch and the danger in the air.

Nobody was home at Bramblewine. After leaving her fourth message on their answering machine, Luna figured that Grandy and Grampy must have gone on a vacation somewhere. Her grandparents had lots of zest for vacations, especially for places where they could play golf.

She hung up the phone and turned her attention to the "Luna's News" Web update. Lots of parents had e-mailed Luna about how much they enjoyed "Luna's News," and some of them had asked her for personal updates about their daughters. Also, the campers themselves liked to be singled out for their special talents. Luna did the best she could, recording the scores of games and keeping track of when a girl had done something exceptional.

There's never a dull moment here at Camp Bliss, she typed. Blue-and-Buff Day is tomorrow, so we are spending plenty of time outdoors preparing for this exciting sports event. Yesterday, **Anne Chapman** caught the most Frisbees in the practice tournament.

"Luna?"

She looked up. Lakshmi stood at the office door.

"Hi, Lakshmi. Are you feeling better?"

Luna asked. Yesterday, Lakshmi had had a bad headache and had spent the day resting in the first-aid office.

"Oh, my head's fine," said Lakshmi. She flopped down in the chair opposite the desk. "I came here because I have something good and something bad to tell you." She smiled. "The good thing is that I came in second place in this morning's two-mile run! Please put that in your Web update."

Luna made a note of it. "And the bad thing?"

Lakshmi frowned and lapsed into silence.

"It couldn't be *that* bad," said Luna in her calm doctor voice.

Lakshmi bit her bottom lip. Her cleft chin trembled slightly. "It's just that you were so nice yesterday, giving me that cold compress for my headache. I have to confess and clear my conscience." She took a deep breath. "I stole your nice yellow powder. And I'm very sorry."

"Oh." Luna blinked. "Why did you take it?"

"I guess because I was in a bad mood to be at camp, and it smelled so outdoorsy it cheered me up," Lakshmi answered. "After I took it, I liked the powder so much I *couldn't* give it back to you. Now it's too late, because someone has stolen it from me."

"The powder has been stolen—again?" asked Luna.

"Yep. Poof! It's gone." For a moment, Lakshmi looked irate. "I'm sorry, Luna. I want to give you replacement money for it. I also wondered where I could get some more. It smelled so nice, like flowers, like a field of—"

Luna held up her hand. "Wait a sec—*how* did you use the powder?"

"Why, I'd sprinkle it on after my shower, of course. It's talcum powder, right?"

"And did anything mysterious happen when you used it?" Luna asked.

Lakshmi looked sheepish. "Well . . . it might sound silly, but whenever I used it, my day seemed extra-lucky. It made me feel . . . oh, I don't know . . . it made me feel . . ."

Luna leaned forward. "Zesty?"

"Yes, that's it. Zesty!" Lakshmi's usually loud voice quieted. "Like, anytime I was mad at Pam—and I was pretty mad about the Pillowcase Fund—well, she would just trip and fall down. Just like that! I know she's probably a klutz to begin with, but it seemed to happen on purpose when I wished it! Or once, when I was enjoying Claire's good ghost story, I thought, oh, wouldn't it be great if we had lightning and rain, to make the night extra scary? And remember? It really happened!"

"And then, when you wanted the food to get better . . ." Luna could not help grinning. Thank goodness, the "witch" had been found!

But Lakshmi shook her head. "No. Somebody took the powder from me before the food improved." Her mouth gaped open. "It *is* magic, isn't it? It's wishing powder! That means I tripped Pam! I made the ghost story scarier! Please, Luna, you *have* to tell me where—"

"Oh, no, you've got the wrong idea." Luna quickly dropped her smile. "I was just joking along with you. What you took was plain old ordinary cornmeal foot powder. You must have been imagining your luck. On the bright side, my grandmother would call that the power of positive thinking! But thanks for telling me. I'd been wondering where my foot powder went. My feet haven't been the same." She stood up from the desk. "Now I've got to find my sister."

Leaving Lakshmi behind, Luna ran out of the office as fast as she could to the pasture, where Claire was practicing archery, a few last-minute bull's-eyes before Blue-and-Buff Day. Claire dropped her bow when Luna gave her the news.

"Then who do you think stole the Zest from Lakshmi?" she asked.

"Someone who likes crunchy tacos and chewy lemon squares," Luna answered.

"Well, we know who that is! Let's go!"

Together, they ran across the field and up near the cabins to the hammock, Penelope's favorite spot, where she was catching a catnap. She confessed immediately.

"Yes, I took the powder from Lakshmi's

shower kit. But I only had it for a couple of days," Penelope said sheepishly. "It smelled so good, like my favorite spices. I couldn't resist. Since Lakshmi hadn't given to the Pillowcase Fund, I figured I'd borrow it and lend it to someone else. I used it as seasoning. It made my food so tasty that I sneaked into the kitchen and sprinkled it in the soup, on the tacos, the chili, even on some stale lemon squares. I couldn't believe one little seasoning could do so much! What's it made of?"

"It's plain old cornmeal foot powder," said Luna.

"Foot powder! Wow! You have to tell me where you got it," said Penelope. "It sure had a lot of zest. I gave the bottle to Gladriole. Since she's a vegetarian and all, I thought she might like an extra kick in her salads. If you want to talk to her, I think she's in the pottery shed."

"Crow's feet and cobwebs!" Claire exclaimed as the twins ran to the pottery shed. "I had no idea that *everyone* at Camp Bliss was casting spells."

"Not *casting*, exactly," corrected Luna. "Just *wishing*."

"That Marigold Zest is powerful stuff," said Claire.

"Grandy warned me not to let the powder get into the wrong hands. She said Marigold Zest could work wonders on even a non-witch's wishes. Now I think I know what she meant." Luna blew out her cheeks. "Boy, did I ever mess this one up."

"Come on, nothing terrible has happened, Loon. None of these wrong hands have been too wrong."

"Not yet, anyway," Luna answered. She shivered. The closer they came to finding the powder, the nearer she felt to a peculiar kind of danger.

Glad was sitting in the windowsill of the pottery barn. She was embroidering a gladiolus design onto a denim cloth wallet.

"Penelope's power powder? Oh, sure! I had it for a couple of days. But I didn't use it on my food! I sprinkled it on my hair before campfire nights, so everyone could share the scent. It gave off a supercool vibe in the air."

"Do you think we could use some of it?" asked Luna.

"Sure! Yesterday, I put it in the Pillowcase Fund for everyone to share."

"Thanks, Glad," said Claire.

"By the way, Luna, I made the longest daisy chain in freestyle crafts time. You might want to put that in your 'Luna's News' update," said Glad.

"Will do," Luna answered.

In no time, the girls had doubled back to Sleepy Hollow. They raced to the pillowcase.

The only thing to be found in the Pillowcase Fund was the copy of *Eternally Eustacia* that Luna had donated.

Claire stamped her foot. "So close, but no Zest! And Camp Bliss is too big to question everybody."

"Hmm, but think, Clairsie. If the powder fulfills the wish of whoever has her hands on it," said Luna thoughtfully, "all we have to do is wait for the next wish, and trace it to the logical wish-er. Right?"

"Right," Claire said softly.

"Like, if everyone starts laughing really hard or wants to play softball all day, then it's Min Suh who has the Zest. Right?"

"Right," squeaked Claire, even more softly.

"Or if people start talking about Bermuda and French manicures too much, then it's Haley who has the Zest. Right?"

"Right." Now Claire's voice sounded soft and squeaky as a mouse.

"Claire, this is no time for funny voices," Luna said strictly. "I'm trying to do some detectiving. Speak up, and stand up straight."

"I am speaking up and standing up!"

Luna looked at her sister from head to toe. "Clairsie," she said, trying to keep her own voice relaxed. "Do you realize that you're shrinking?"

"I am not!" said Claire, jutting her chin high. Yet there could be no doubt that she was standing a full head smaller than her sister. And she was losing height rapidly.

"What is happening to you?" Luna

gasped. Now her sister was at her chest, and in the next ten seconds, her waist.

"Make it stop!" Claire commanded. Her voice was shrill as a doll's teakettle.

"I don't know how!" Luna cried. Now her twin was knee-high. "You're knee-high!" she exclaimed, but no sooner were the words out than Claire had shrunk to Luna's shin, then her ankle. "Claire, where are you going?"

"Hide me!" squealed Claire, climbing up onto Luna's big toe. "Put me somewhere safe, before I disappear from sight!"

Quickly, Luna scooped up her clothespin-sized sister and dropped her gently into a paper cup that was resting on top of one of the bureaus. "We'll go to the first-aid office," she said. "Stay calm. Either you have come down with an incurable shrinking disease, or a rebel wisher has struck."

She hurried out of the cabin and down the hill to the office, the safest place she could think of. She peeked in the cup. "Crumbs, Clairsie, you're teeny! Who would be cruel enough to wish you down to the size of a matchstick?"

"I'm much bigger than a matchstick!" Claire peeped haughtily. "Hurry!"

"I'm running as fast as I can!" said Luna. "Let's try to access the Book of Shadows from the Internet. We'll have you back to normal in no time. Now keep quiet, because I see somebody walking up over the hill."

The somebody was Ella Edsel.

"Is that Claire or Luna?" she asked, squinting and shading her eyes.

"Luna," said Luna.

As she got closer, Ella smiled. "Just who I was looking for. By the way, I can tell you from your sister because you have way prettier eyes."

Inside the cup, Claire squeaked with rage.

"Talita sent me to find you," Ella continued. "Your grandmother is calling long distance. You need to get to the office, pronto!"

"Thanks," said Luna. "She's just the person I wanted to talk to."

"By the way, have you seen Claire

around?" Ella smirked. "We've got relay races in fifteen minutes. Last practice before Blue-and-Buff Day tomorrow."

"Um, no," said Luna. "But I'm looking for something, too. I wanted to borrow some yellow powder from the Pillowcase Fund. Have you seen it?"

"You mean that foot powder? Too late now," Ella answered. "I used it all up on my feet. It feels great, like I have extra kicking energy! That's why I know for sure that Blue is gonna win!"

Now Claire let out a squeak so loud and angry that Luna had to fake a sneeze to cover up the noise.

"Hope you're not getting a cold before Blue-and-Buff Day," said Ella. "By the way, Luna, make sure to add in your news bulletin that I kicked the winning goal in soccer practice."

"No problem," said Luna.

"Nothing personal, but I'm gonna blow your sister away tomorrow!" Ella cackled. "In my opinion, she's no more than a little flea!"

8

Tug-of-Warriors

CLAIRE COULD HEAR that Grandy was annoyed. She was talking on her cell phone from a golf course somewhere in the Poconos. "What did I say about not letting the powder fall into the wrong hands?" she yelled. Claire covered her ears. Now that she was flea-sized, all voices sounded loud as thunder.

"I'm sorry," answered Luna. "Grandy, this is a real mess. Claire's smaller than a paper clip. Ella Edsel wished it, and her wish is coming true!"

"Nice one, Fred!" shouted Grandy. "That's two birdies and a hole in one!"

"When will the wish wear off?" Claire yelled, jumping up and down in the paper cup. The sound of her voice was hardly a sound at all. Luckily, Grandy's ears were better than a bat's.

"A non-witch's wish? Ha! It's a joke, it takes absolutely nothing to undo," said Grandy. "And it's not permanent, anyway. Luna can restore you to regular size on a pinkie spell. As for that girl, Ella, and her extra kicking energy, that's where you have a problem. As you two have learned, Marigold Zest is a non-witch-friendly powder, and since Ella correctly shook the Zest on her feet, she'll probably be the star of any sport where she needs a good, strong, zesty kick. If perchance she faced west, her power would be even greater."

Claire felt tears sting as her mind's eye imagined Ella Edsel zestfully kicking goal after goal. Good-bye, Buff Team Victory! Good-bye, loving cup!

Mostly, though, Claire wanted to be the right size again.

"Grandy, I hate being puny!" she yelled as loud as she could. "Make me grow back before Ella squashes me like a flea!"

"Buck up, Claire. Terrible things happen to people every day, and you don't hear them squeaking on and on about it." But then Grandy quickly recited a "return-to-size" spell for Luna to cast on her sister. "Listen, girls. The reason I'm calling is to tell you I arranged for your father and Justin to pick you two up next week," she announced. "Foolishly, they think it might be a fun road trip! Oh, Fred, gorgeous shot! Now, remember. Absolutely No More Spells! Hugs and kisses! Good-bye!"

Claire heard Luna send a kiss and replace the phone.

"Hurry, Loon!" she squeaked, hopping up and down. How big was a flea, anyway? A centimeter? A millimeter? Awful Ella Edsel!

"Luna, if your cup is empty, come toss it in this bag." From somewhere in the room came Talita's voice. Claire strained through the cup to see Talita's shadowy outline in the office door. "I'm taking the trash up to the lodge."

Claire felt Luna's fingers close around the cup protectively.

"Okay," said Luna. "Let me just, um . . ." And then, before Claire could squeak in protest, she felt herself being lifted and shaken forward, sliding from the cup where she landed—yuck!—in the damp warm cave of Luna's mouth. It was dark as midnight and smelled like peanut butter. Claire perched herself on her sister's right front molar and pinched her nose against the peanut-butter fumes.

"Bye, then," Talita called. "Don't forget to turn off the computer."

"Mmmggrlk," Luna answered.

"Open up!" Claire shouted, her teensy sneaker kicking the edge of Luna's tongue. "It's hot in here! Sitting in your after-lunch mouth is beyond blecchh!"

Gently, she felt herself being spit from dark to light to land on the pink island of Luna's palm. Then Luna crouched to let Claire drop to the ground, where she scrambled to stand on her own two tiny legs.

"Sorry about that. It was the only place I

could think of to hide you. Now, sister-witch, be thou ready?"

Claire nodded. "Aye."

She looked up and watched as Luna's enormous pinkie hovered over her like a rain cloud as she cast:

Undo this curse of cruel despise
Return Claire to her natural size.
It's only logical to me,
My sister cannot be a flea!

Slowly, Claire felt herself stretching and pulling and shaping back into her regular old self.

"What a relief!" she said when she stood eye to eye and was the same size as her sister, the way it had been since Claire could remember. "I'll never look at a flea the same way again. Or your mouth. Pee-yew, Luna! You should brush after lunch. You've got me smelling like a peanut-butter-and-bad-breath sandwich!"

Luna frowned. "There are more important things to think about than how you smell. You have Ella Edsel to compete against, and her feet are zesty."

"I understand how rebel witches turned out to be rebel *wishers*. But what I still don't get," Claire said as they began to walk up to Sleepy Hollow, "is who did the apple spell?"

"Apple spell? What apple spell?" asked Luna.

"I didn't want to scare you, Loon, but a few weeks ago, I found an apple quartered and buried right outside Sleepy Hollow. You and I both know that's an Old School, problem-solving spell. That's why I *still* think Ella Edsel might be a real-live, sneaky rebel witch."

Luna cleared her throat. "Actually, Claire, the apple-caster was me. It was just this dumb thing I did my first week here, when I hate-hate-hated Camp Bliss. I knew Grandy had said No Spells, but an apple spell has almost no magic at all. I told my problem to the apple because I didn't want to tell you. I didn't want to wreck your fun."

"You like camp now, though, right?" Claire asked.

Luna nodded. "It took longer, but I guess there's a place for me here, too."

Claire threw her arm around her sister. "Of course there is! I'm proud of you, Loon. You're not a great athlete, but you're a great sport."

Luna threw her arm around Claire. "Good luck tomorrow," she said. "I know you'll be terrific. You have all the zest you need, with or without spells. I'm pulling for you."

"You better pull for me," Claire said soberly. "You're on my team. Together, we've got to make the extra effort to crush Ella."

Claire kept away from Ella for the rest of the evening. She did not even bother to go out to Cow Patty pasture to watch how far Ella could kick the soccer ball. "Luna's right. I don't need magic zest," she whispered to herself. "I've got enough zest in me already."

The next morning dawned bright and muggy, with a light wind off Lake Periwinkle. The camp was set up for a day of competition. The fields had been mowed, and the air smelled like the fresh, clean, blue and buff T-shirts that had been ordered especially for Blue-and-Buff Day.

"Go, Buff, go!" Claire called to anyone she saw in a Buff Team shirt.

"That's the spirit, Claire!" said Tammy.

Everything was going to be okay, Claire decided. Spirit was practically the same thing as zest.

At breakfast, though, Claire saw that Ella had pulled her hair into two pom-pom pony-tails, and she had painted her face with blue stripes.

"I am Big Bad Blue!" Ella sang zestfully. "I am True Blue!"

"Great spirit!" Tammy, Pam, and Talita declared. Some of the older girls from Cabin Eight whistled and clapped approvingly.

Claire wished she had thought to paint her face buff or make a pom-pom hairdo. If she did it now, she would look like a copycat.

After breakfast, Glad lent her a tan bandanna, which she tied around her head. Then she wrote *Tuff Enuff for Buff* on her leg, using a yellow glow-paint pen.

"Oooh! Let me try!" The other girls on the

team borrowed the paint pen to write on their legs, too.

"Great slogan, Claire! Good leadership!" called the counselors as the entire camp assembled on the field, waiting for the games to start.

Pam strode to the head of the group and lifted her whistle. "Sports fans! The all-day sports-athon known as Blue-and-Buff Day has officially begun. Get set for some volleyball action!" Then she put her mouth on the whistle, puffed out her cheeks, and gave the loudest, longest, screechingest blast yet.

The teams divided. Two volleyball games, one on the North Court, one on the South Court, would be played at the same time. That way, everyone had a chance to participate. Claire and Ella were both on the North Court.

Claire's eyebrows raised, and her mouth buttoned in determination as she and Ella faced off across the net.

"Blue's ups!" Ella shouted. But then she only served an easy pop-up that Claire slammed down the middle.

"All right!" cheered the Buff team.

Ella scowled and served again.

Again, Claire slammed a return into the ground.

"Yes!" cheered Buff.

"Be a team player, Claire!" yelled Pam.

Ella served once more, and the ball went out of bounds.

"Out! Out! Out! Yer out! Buff's ups! Our serve!" shouted Claire.

Blue-and-Buff Day was underway.

In every event, Claire and Ella were neck and neck. If Claire got a bull's-eye in archery, Ella leaped farther in the long jump. If Ella did an extra chin-up, Claire shaved a second off her relay time.

"True Blue!" Ella crowed as she slammed a grounder between second and third base during the softball game.

"Tuff Buff!" Claire shouted back when she slung and shot her third bull's-eye in the archery competition.

They kept their eyes on each other, waiting to see who would break the truce and cheat. As far as Claire could see, Ella was playing as honestly as she was playing zestfully. Now that she was charged with the extra zing of magic zest, Ella seemed to be more agreeable to rules and fairness. Well, of course, thought Claire grimly. Anyone would be a good sport if she had magically zesty feet!

A chalkboard had been set up by Wuthering Heights cabin. Every time Claire checked on it, the Buff Team was either up by one or down by one. Sometimes Ella swooped by to check, too.

"You're toast!" Claire would hiss.

"Takes one to know one," Ella hissed back.

"Ella Edsel and Claire Bundkin! Stop checking the board," Pam called. "Just enjoy the competition."

Enjoy it? Impossible!

The Buff Team won the rope climb. The Blue Team won capture the flag. The Buff Team won the softball game. The Blue Team won the canoe relay, which was to be expected since Luna was the worst canoer ever to paddle Lake Periwinkle. (But Claire was truly proud of Luna during the canoe relays. Although she wore two life jackets and did not open her eyes the whole time she was on the water, Luna paddled all the way to the finish line.)

The last event of Blue-and-Buff Day was the tug-of-war. Talita tallied the scores on the board. "If Buff wins," she announced to the group, "this day ends in a tie. Then two flags will fly over Camp Bliss. If Blue wins, then the blue flag will fly alone for another year!"

"Tuff Buff!" screamed Tammy.

"True Blue!" screamed Pam.

"Tuggers, take your places!" Pam's breath could barely fill the whistle as she blew into it. Everyone was splattered, battered, muddied, bruised, and beyond exhausted. Some of the Cabin One campers had quit the day long ago and were taking naps in the hammock.

Claire jumped to the head of line. She picked up the rope and gripped it firmly. A red handkerchief was tied around the middle of the rope to mark its dividing point. "Come on," she whispered to the handkerchief. "A victory for Buff is a victory for me!"

Across the black goo of a lumpy mud puddle created by the counselors just for the tug, Claire stared into the eyes of a very sweaty Ella. Only faint smears of blue streaked her face now, and she had lost one of her pompoms, which made her look lopsided. Claire knew that she herself was looking pretty messy, too. The yellow glow-paint down her leg had smudged into a bruise-y color, and her lower lip was swollen from biting it too hard during the rope climb.

"Forget about winning, Lice Monger Queen of All Cooties," Claire growled with what energy was left in her. "The Buff Team flag will fly."

"In your dreams, Puny Pitiful Fleabite," puffed Ella. "The Blue Team flag flies high and alone!"

Pam blew her whistle, and the tugging began.

Claire pulled. Her arms strained so hard she thought she could feel her joints popping out of her sockets, but she didn't care. All that mattered was winning. She tugged as hard as she could. Ella tugged hard, too. She stomped her zesty feet so that mud kicked up everywhere, spattering Claire's face. Claire stomped her own feet and spattered back.

The handkerchief i n c h e d over the mud puddle.

And i n c h e d its way back.

That's when it happened. Maybe because of Ella's lopsided pom-pom hair. Maybe because of her puffing, blue-smudged face. Maybe because of her giant, mud-spattered, zesty feet that were stuck like two scuba flippers in the mud. Maybe it was a combination of all three things. But suddenly, Ella Edsel looked very, very funny to Claire.

So funny that Claire felt something like a giant hiccup rising from her stomach. She tried to stop it by gritting her teeth. She pulled with all her might.

The handkerchief i n c h e d closer to the Blue Team side.

"Pull, Blue, pull!" she heard Pam yell.

"Pull, Buff, pull!" yelled Tammy.

Ella was glaring at Claire. Her face was fierce, but she seemed to be holding back an uncomfortable, hiccup-y expression as well. Did Claire look as fierce to Ella as Ella did to Claire?

"Mmm-mmm-mmm!" Ella started to make a noise in the back of her throat.

"Mmm-mmm-mmm!" Claire could not push the hiccup down.

It was impossible, later, for the counselors to decide who let go of the rope first. But as soon as Ella and Claire both lost their grip, everyone else did, too. In a confused instant, the line slammed sideways, skidding into the mud. Girls tumbled and slid into one another before being sucked down into sloppy, gooey mud.

Ella and Claire, who landed plop in the middle of the mud puddle, were holding their stomachs from laughing so hard.

"True Blue!" wheezed Claire.

"Tuff Enough!" Ella gasped.

Blue-and-Buff Day was officially over.

Mr. and Mrs. Carol, the camp directors, who had come to watch the last hour of Blue-

and-Buff Day, ruled that the tug-of-war would not be counted in the official tally.

"And so the winner is—the Blue Team!" announced Pam at the pizza and root-beer-float celebration afterward. "The Blue Flag will fly another year! Hip, hip, hooray!"

As the counselors saluted the flag, all of the blue-shirted girls cheered and clapped. The buff-shirted girls clapped, too, but more quietly.

Claire gave Ella a nudge and raised up her root-beer mug in a toast.

"You played really great today," she admitted.

"You, too. You're a terrific athlete," confessed Ella.

"Takes one to know one!" shouted Claire, and they clinked mugs on it.

9
The End of Bliss

"**B**OO!" THE VOICE at the lodge door was low and rumbly. At first, Luna did not recognize it. She jumped, startled, and dropped her Ping-Pong paddle.

"Justin!" She hardly recognized her brother. He had become so tall. And dark. And handsome.

"What happened to you?" she exclaimed.

Justin looked shy. Then, catching sight of Lakshmi at the other end of the Ping-Pong table, he recovered by pulling up his shirt-sleeve and flexing a muscle. Two hard bumps appeared. "I made a wad of money, too," he said in his low and rumbling new voice.

"That's great, Justin."

"Dad let me drive part of the way here. On the back roads." Now his voice was extra loud, too.

"That's cool, Justin."

"I'm Justin," said Justin, turning to Lakshmi.

"I'm Lakshmi," said Lakshmi in her own loud voice, stepping forward. "I'm from Los Angeles."

"Yeah, I've been there," said Justin. Luna was about to remind him that he had been to Los Angeles when he was six months old and probably couldn't remember a single thing about it, but the look on his face made her stop.

"Dad and I are staying at the Mossy Minute Motel," Justin continued loudly. He was looking at Luna, but his sneakers were pointed in Lakshmi's direction. "We did a road trip. It was so great. We had fish gumbo at this place in Baltimore. We toured around Roanoke, and we visited a cowboy museum. I drove part of the way on the back roads."

"You told us that already," Luna reminded him.

"Driving is cool," said Lakshmi. "I can't wait to get my license. Are you in high school?"

"Ymm-hmm," said Justin, giving Luna another look that made her decide not to remind him that he was actually starting eighth grade in September, and last she checked, eighth grade was not high school.

Loudly, Justin continued, speaking more to Lakshmi than Luna. "We'll be at the cook-out and your awards ceremony tonight, and I call the front passenger seat for tomorrow. I'm gonna go find Claire and say hi to her, too. See ya."

He ducked out of the lodge, red-faced from so much talking.

"Your brother's cool," Lakshmi commented. "Does he have a girlfriend?"

"I don't think so," said Luna. She had a

feeling that underneath her new, brawny, loud-talking, muscled-up brother was the same shy, girlfriendless Justin. "I'm going to go look for my dad."

She did not have to go far. Mr. Bundkin was striding up the field in search of her.

At the sight of her father's friendly, familiar face, a tide of happiness and homesickness and car sickness and top-bunk sickness surged through her. Luna felt tears prickle in her eyes. She pretended that she had to sneeze so that she could cover her face with her hands.

"Thanks for posting those 'Luna's News' updates," Mr. Bundkin said, swooping up Luna for a hug and a kiss. "You make a great scout reporter!"

"I'm happy to see you," said Luna, sagging into her father's shoulder. Five weeks had been a long time, she realized. She was ready to go. Camp Bliss had been kind of fun, but she'd had to work really hard at it. Now she wanted to be home in her own room in her own bed with her own kitten purring on the end of it.

Mr. Bundkin wasn't the only one to thank

Luna for her news updates. All afternoon and later that evening at the Farewell Picnic, parents came up to shake her hand. "Luna Bundkin? Nice bulletin! We really appreciated the reports from the front lines!"

The attention from grown-ups was all a little bit embarrassing, especially when Talita introduced Luna to her boyfriend, Curtis, as "my best friend at camp."

Which was sort of true, thought Luna as she watched Talita and Curtis sitting together under a tree, sharing a plate of picnic dinner and whispering secrets. She and Talita had even exchanged e-mail addresses. But Curtis was Talita's all-weather friend. They were traveling across Europe together next year. Talita had told her all about it.

Sitting next to her father, Luna nibbled at her dinner and surveyed the rolling green fields. Everywhere she looked, she saw a pair of friends.

Glad and Penelope were sitting together.
Min Suh and Haley were sitting together.
Pam and Tammy were sitting together.

Even Lakshmi and Justin were sitting together.

"I can't believe camp's over," said Luna quietly, "and I never made an all-weather friend."

"You're my all-weather friend," said her father. "Right, sunshine?"

Luna nodded and put her hand on his knee. She didn't want her dad to feel bad, but a parent wasn't quite the same thing. Besides, she really was happy to see her dad after five weeks away from him.

Since it was such a warm, clear evening, the Camp Bliss awards ceremony would be held outdoors. On a flat stretch of meadow, folding chairs were arranged in rows. Up front, a table covered with badges, medals, and certificates was positioned next to a podium. After dinner, people began to amble over from the barbecue area to sit on the chairs. Luna waited for her dad to finish his third helping of potato salad, then held his hand as they joined the others.

"Justin and I will be back here, a stone's throw away," said Mr. Bundkin, detaching his hand from hers. "You go sit with the other kids, Luna."

Claire and Ella had saved her a seat up front. Luna felt her stomach clench with jealousy. Even Claire had made an all-weather friend! Ever since Blue-and-Buff Day, Claire and Ella had become inseparable.

Luna managed to put on a smile as she trotted down the aisle to slide into the empty seat next to her sister.

Ella leaned forward and waved. Claire hooked her pinkie into Luna's. Then Talita spied Luna, and she and Curtis moved seats so that they could sit next to her.

"Look at that loving cup," Claire said, pointing. "If Ella and I both win it, then we decided we each will hold one of its handles. I think there's a reason it has two handles. It's *kismet*."

"What's kismet?" Luna asked.

"Destiny!" said Claire and Ella together. Then they started laughing. Ever since Claire and Ella had become friends, it seemed all they did was laugh.

Soon Pam and the other counselors gathered at the front. As she stepped into place behind the podium, Pam blew on her whistle. But it was a mournful *tweet*, as if she knew it would be a whole year before she would use a whistle so much and so happily again.

"There are lots of prizes to give out," Pam announced to the audience. "Your patience is appreciated! We're going to start with the junior campers crafts awards and tadpole badges. Okay?"

"Dandy!" shouted a few campers.

Pam grinned.

There were prizes for everything. There were ribbons and badges and medallions for good swimming, for good sailing, for good art-work, for good hiking and biking and Frisbee and horseshoe tossing. Everyone won some-thing, and any girl who didn't win a prize was named for an honorable mention. Even Luna's name was called (for passing the first aid test). Of course, most of the time Ella and Claire were the ones who jumped up to sprint down the aisle. Soon their laps were filled with paper, cloth, and metal honors.

Luna's hands hurt from clapping. Her sister was amazing!

How would that trophy be split between Claire and Ella? Luna stared at the big silver cup and pondered. Would Claire get it for half the year and Ella for half the year? Would they flip a coin? Would another cup have to be made?

Eventually, the table lay bare, except for the trophy. A hush fell over the crowd.

Claire leaned forward. Ella leaned forward. The audience shifted forward.

Then Pam sat down. Mr. and Mrs. Carol, who had been sitting in the front row of the audience, now stood up and took Pam's place at the podium. Mrs. Carol then began to read in a clear, slow voice.

"The loving cup is given to the camper who represents those qualities most important to Camp Bliss," she began. "They are loyalty, sportsmanship, enterprise, and bravery. This year, the counselors told me they had a tough job. There were so many outstanding competitors. So many winners!"

Someone shouted out Claire's name.

Someone else shouted Ella's. Then someone shouted Julianna Becker's, who won it last year but who was not even at camp this year. Then everyone was yelling out any name.

Pam blew on her whistle. Mr. Carol raised his hand for quiet. The noise settled.

"This year, we decided to give the award to a camper who made an unusual contribution," Mr. Carol continued. "This camper got to know everyone through her hard work both indoors and out. Whether she was taking out splinters or paddling a canoe, she was always testing her *bravery*. Her interest in other campers resulted in an *enterprising* newsletter available online to all Bliss parents. She participated with steady and enthusiastic *sportsmanship* in every sport, and she *loyally* befriended both counselors and campers alike."

Now Mr. and Mrs. Carol spoke together. "That is why this year's Camp Bliss Girl award goes to Luna Bundkin."

A hush of surprise fell over the audience, followed by a murmuring. It was instantly replaced by quiet, then steady clapping.

"Lizards and love handles!" whispered Claire. "Loon?"

"Oh, no!" Luna whispered. She scrunched down in her seat. "I can't!"

The applause was gaining strength. A few girls began to shout Luna's name. From somewhere in the back, Luna heard Justin give a wolf howl.

Claire turned and hugged her. "I guess you do deserve it, Luna," she whispered in her sister's ear. "I never thought about it that way before, but you really do have all those loving-cup qualities!"

"But I can't walk up in front of all those people," Luna whispered back. "My legs are shaking from nerves. Will you do it for me? Please? It was your zest for adventure that made me come to Camp Bliss in the first place. You're the whole reason I'm here!"

Claire looked at Luna.

Luna looked at Claire.

"Are you sure?" Claire whispered.

Luna nodded. She was sure.

While most of the campers half-knew that it was Claire, not Luna, Bundkin who stood up and walked down the aisle and up to the podium to shake hands with the Carols and the counselors and accept the big two-handled silver trophy, it did not matter. Everyone knew that Luna and Claire, though they were as different as chalk and cheese, could count on each other in a pinch. That was why they were the purest kind of identical twins.

"See? Kismet," said Claire later, after Justin and their dad had left for the motel, and they took one final tour around the campgrounds. "I even cleared a space for the loving cup on our bookshelf. So we both can admire it."

Luna looked at the cup. Camp Bliss Girl—her! She could hardly believe it. "You're sure you're not sad you didn't win it?" she asked her sister.

"I'm a little sad," admitted Claire. "But, then again, Ella and I had a lot of fun together. Even though you won the trophy, camp is still a more perfect place for kids like Ella and me. Fun-wise, that is."

"I agree," Luna said.

"And it might have been kind of bad if just I or Ella won. Do you know that she invited us to spend a week with her in Colorado? There's a horse farm nearby, and we'll be able to ride horses all day. Isn't that cool?"

"Yes," said Luna with a smile. "You know what, Claire? Even though it was you who made an all-weather friend, and I who won the loving cup, it doesn't make a difference in the end. We both lucked out, a double victory."

"And we split the profits down the middle," said Claire, planting a big smooch on the loving cup and leaving greasy lip-marks, which Luna carefully wiped away.

The next morning, there were many good-byes and hugs and e-mails and numbers exchanged. Clothing trunks were packed into car trunks, and the twins fastened into their seat belts. The empty vial of Marigold Zest clanked inside the trophy cup between them.

"It's still five bucks a pop for me to carry those trunks up to your rooms," Justin reminded them, speaking in a braggy way for Lakshmi's benefit.

Lakshmi smiled. "Hey, Justin," she said so quietly that the twins had to strain their ears to listen in. "Send me an e-mail as soon as you get home. But remember, you're three hours ahead of California."

"Sure thing." Justin smiled shyly.

Claire put her hands around her throat and made a gagging noise, and as soon as Justin hopped in the car, he reached behind to smack her.

It was back to old times again.

As Mr. Bundkin pulled out of the parking lot, Ella galloped alongside the car, pretending that she was riding a horse.

"Good-bye! So long!" she shouted to Claire. "Promise you won't forget me! Remember to write!"

"I promise! I'll remember!" Claire shouted back.

The twins looked out the back window,

waving, and watched as Ella's red hair and the peaked fir trees of Camp Bliss shrank to nothing. Eventually all they could see was the speck of the flapping blue flag.

"Next year, I'll change that flag color," Claire resolved. "When we come back to Bliss. Right, Luna?"

Luna nodded. Right.